PURITY

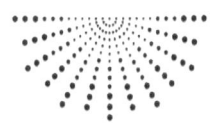

DOUGLAS CLEGG

ALKEMARA
PRESS

GET THE NEWSLETTER

Get book updates, exclusive offers, news of contests & special treats for readers—become a V.I.P. member of Douglas Clegg's long-running free newsletter at http://DouglasClegg.com/newsletter

ALSO BY DOUGLAS CLEGG

STAND-ALONE NOVELS

NOVELLAS & SHORT NOVELS

The Necromancer

The Words

SERIES

THE HARROW SERIES

Nightmare House, Book 1

Mischief, Book 2

The Infinite, Book 3

The Abandoned, Book 4

The Necromancer (Prequel Novella)

Isis (Prequel Novella)

THE CRIMINALLY INSANE SERIES

Bad Karma, Book 1

Red Angel, Book 2

Night Cage, Book 3

THE VAMPYRICON TRILOGY

The Priest of Blood, Book 1

The Lady of Serpents, Book 2

The Queen of Wolves, Book 3

THE CHRONICLES OF MORDRED

Mordred, Bastard Son (Book 1)

Mordred, Dragon Prince (Book 2)

COLLECTIONS

Lights Out: Collected Stories

Night Asylum

The Nightmare Chronicles

Wild Things

BOX SET BUNDLES

Bad Places (3 Novels)

Coming of Age (3 Dark Novellas)

Dark Rooms (3 Novels)

Criminally Insane: The Series (3 Novels)

Halloween Chillers

Harrow: Three Novels (Books 1-3)

Harrow: Four Novels (Books 1-4)

Haunts (8 Novel Box Set)

Lights Out (3 Collection Box Set)

Night Towns (3 Novels)

The Vampyricon Trilogy (3 Novels)

With more new novels, novellas and stories to
come.

For Raul

PURITY

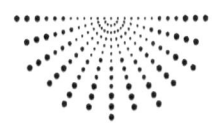

"Vast, Polyphemus-like, and loathsome, it darted like a stupendous monster of nightmares…" —*H.P. Lovecraft, from "Dagon."*

SUMMER BEGINS

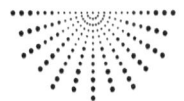

WHY I CALLED YOU HERE

There is no madness but the madness of the gods. There is no purity but the purity of love.

SOMEONE ONCE WROTE that "the most merciful thing in the world, I think, is the inability of the human mind to correlate its contents."

This sentiment describes my feelings perfectly. I correlate too much of my own mind's contents. It's always troubling. I don't live in the chronological moment; I doubt you do, either. I live all at once in the past with only glimpses of the present. I live mostly on that island, when it comes to me, when I think of my life as it formed. I live in darkness now, but the dark brings the memories back. The dark brings it all back. The dark is all I know. I call the dark. It's there that I find the god I met one day when I was just a child. I remember that day; not the days of blood to come. In the end, we were together.

In the beginning, we were not.

HERE ARE the words I will never forget:

"Owen, I'm so sorry. I'm so sorry. I should never have come this summer."

Before that, the gun went off.

Before that, I looked into her eyes.

Before that is when it all began.

Dagon, bring it back to me.

WHO I AM

These are the things I know: Outerbridge Island has briny water running beneath its rocks, a subterranean series of narrow channels between the Sound and the Atlantic. You can see the entrances to these channels on the northern side of the island at low tide.

These channels feed into the Great Salt Pond on the westerly side of the island before it empties into the sea. It was said that once upon a time, a Dutch trading ship smashed up against the rocks, and local pirates fed upon the treasures found within the hold of the ship. The treasure, it is said, was buried in the narrow caverns. To add to the chill of this tale, it was also said that the pirates fed upon the flesh of the survivors of the wreck for days.

I've actually swum into the caverns at times. I'm slender enough, and in good enough shape to maneuver in the darkness of the water, but I never found treasure, nor did I emerge in the Great Salt Pond by following the channels within that part of the island. I needed air, after all.

If you want something badly enough, there are ways to get it.

This doesn't mean they are traditional means. It doesn't mean that pain is not involved. It doesn't mean that the cost may not overwhelm the need. It just means there are ways to get what you really want in this world.

If one has a conscience, one can be driven mad. Therefore, a conscience is a key to madness. Everyone is a potential madman. Everyone. The sweetest boy in the world can be driven to the most irrational of acts. The girl who has the world at her feet, likewise, could be pushed toward some act of desperation and tragedy.

And, in many ways, we want the irrational and the tragic and the desperate, because they bring meaning and life back into our existences.

Another fact: My mother prizes three things above all others.

First, the rose garden which my father

planted for her before I was born. It runs in spirals along the bluffs and the small hillock behind our cottage. There are fourteen varieties of roses, with hues ranging from pale peach to blood red.

Second, her koi pond, which is really the Montgomerys' koi pond, but it sits on our side of the property. It is largish for a pond, and narrow, nearly a reflecting pool. It was built deep for the harsh winters—the koi can survive a thick layer of ice as long as they can bury themselves down in the silt. My father covers the pool with a plastic tarp to further protect the fish.

And finally, my mother prizes the gun. My maternal grandfather had a pistol that had been given to him by his mother.

It was a small Colt pistol—what my grandfather called a vest pistol, but which I thought of as a Saturday Night Special. It had mother-of-pearl grips, and a clip that could not be removed from it.

My grandfather had given my mother the pistol in the early years of her marriage to protect herself when my father would beat her. My father never beat my mother, but my grandfather would apparently not believe it. The pistol is useless, I heard my mother once say. Never been fired. I could barely shoot a cat with it, she joked.

Someday, she told me, when she was weepy and bitter about life, she would go to Boston and sell it to a collector and take the money and go far, far away.

When I first discovered my true god and his nature, I took the pistol.

Final fact: Faith plays into all of this. One must have faith that one can do what one sets out to do. One must have the courage of one's convictions. All the world's history teaches us this.

For me, it is that god I discovered. I call it Dagon, although its name is unknown to me. It came from the sea, and I held it captive, briefly.

I am its priest. And Dagon, in a twisted and true way, upholds what I stand for.

One must stand for something.

For me, it is the force of love. The undertow of love. But that sounds romantic, and I'm not a romantic at all. I've been called a lot of things since the day I was born, but never romantic. Schemer. Athlete. Brain. Manipulator. User. Common. Handsome. Shallow. Arrogant. Mad. Sociopath. Cold eyes. All by my mother.

Jenna Montgomery once told me I had the most beautiful eyes she'd ever seen on a boy.

I had to catch my breath when she told me that.

She said it the same day I made the first sacrifice to the god I'd met.

YEARS AGO, I came upon the god during a storm of late November, a frozen, bitter storm, in which I had gotten caught down at the caverns, taking a dinghy out to look for the famous buried pirate treasure.

I was twelve and lonely, and when I saw the god thrust in between a rock and a hard place, as it were, I knew immediately who and what it was, and how I should please it. I read in my father's bible that Dagon was the god of the Philistines; the Fish-God. I found other books, too, with titles like *The Shadow over Innsmouth* and *Dagon,* that further told of the god and its worshippers and what was needed to feed the god.

Some may say it is just an abominable statue, a cheap and even grotesque trinket of some distant bazaar, brought by sailors or perhaps even the pirates. It is green with age, and made wholly of stone. Its eyes are merely garnet; its tail and fins carved with some exquisite artistry.

But when I bled a seagull over the cold eyes of the little god, while the storm raged around me, I felt a prayer had been answered. I breathed easier then.

BREATHING IS ESSENTIAL TO SURVIVAL, and although this seems like a given, we know—scientifically—that it is not. Most of the problems of life are like that: simple, obvious, graspable, yet shrouded in a secret.

If one can breathe well—through any crisis, and exertion—then one will survive. It is those who stop breathing who have let go of their wills to live. I am what people in this world call a sociopath, although the idea of killing someone has never interested me.

A sociopath is not necessarily a killer, and to assume this is to play a dangerous game. Just as not all famous people are rich, not all sociopaths are Jeffrey Dahmer. If Jeffrey was one at all.

You must know this about me if you're going to understand exactly what went on at Outerbridge Island the summer I turned eighteen, the summer before Jenna Montgomery was to leave me forever.

They say that people like me can't experience love, but I find that a ridiculous statement. I'm fully capable of giving and receiving love, and it is monstrous to suggest otherwise. Even all those years ago I was, and love burned in me just as it did any boy who had fallen.

My mother would take her daily pain pill as I grew up—her pains being life itself and even her child—and tell me that there were two kinds of people in this world, the kind that give and the kind that take, and I knew I was neither, but somewhere in between the rest of the world: I was someone who observed, perhaps too coldly at times. I still observe, and observation has brought me to this place again.

Outerbridge Island, with its rocky ledges and glassy sea, the fog that came suddenly, the sun that tore through clouds like a nuclear explosion, the summers that went for years; the years that passed in a summer.

The storms that came and stayed and never left.

LET me turn it all back to the day I was born, since from what I've read about sociopaths, it's a fairly genetic condition.

My grandmother was probably the carrier of the gene, since she went crazy and ended up in what they called a nursing home over in Massachusetts, but which I found out—later in life, of course—was an impoverished sanitarium, the sort from which nightmares are born.

My mother told me it was my grandfather's fault for driving her to do things—again, not kill, for we have never been murderers—just things that caused people to believe my grandmother was insane.

When I was born, as my mother told me when I was eleven or twelve, I presented a difficult birth. My umbilical cord practically strangled me as I exited her body. She said I was blue in the face for nearly a minute from lack of oxygen before the doctor got me coughing. Then, I spent the first two weeks of my life in the hospital, for I was a month premature and no one thought I would live.

Sometimes I think this is why I'm a sociopath. I've seen documentaries on PBS about baby monkeys who are separated from their mothers for a short time, and this makes them seem without conscience (if that is truly what a sociopath is, although I don't believe it). My mother said she didn't touch me for the first month; she was terrified I'd die, and because she had already lost one child—two years earlier—in some kind of crib death incident, she feared holding her first son, me. My father had to do all the touching and picking up, and even—my mother told me—nursing me felt unnatural and dangerous to her. Instead, my aunt became my wet nurse—she who had, just five months before, given birth to twins and seemed to have milk enough for the entire population of the island.

There were times, when I was older, that I wished my aunt had taken me back with her to her home on the mainland. Times when I hated the island. Hated my mother and father. Hated looking at the Montgomery house—the Montgomery Mansion, the Montgomery Palazzo, the Big Place—staring down at us. But I suppose all this anger came about because of those first few days of life.

These things aren't spoken of much in families—how we each came to be. My mother suffered through bouts of depression, particularly in the winter, and she would stand in front of her bedroom window, looking out across the Sound, her face a shimmering reflection in the thick window glass, and tell me all about myself.

She told me that when I was six weeks old, she realized I had never really cried, at least not the way babies were supposed to. Instead, I would turn red, and my mouth would open, and I'd scream. That's how she'd know I was hungry or needed changing. Because she was so grateful to have a child after she felt God had taken away her first in retribution for youthful transgressions, she tried not to think about what my lack of tears might mean.

As she'd tell this kind of story, I'd shift uncomfortably on her bed, wishing she'd release me from this strange intimacy—the closeness of her depression, the morbid way her mind would pick over my birth and early years.

"I'm so sorry that you turned out this way," she said, once, her hands going up to her face. "I'm happy you're so smart. Not like your father. But this madness that comes over you…."

I remained silent, letting her have her feelings. I didn't understand then to what she referred—I was not mad. I took the ferry to go to school over on the mainland and did quite well in school. The ferry takes an hour and a half in the winter, and only runs twice a day—for school hours, since Outerbridge had no school of its own. Thus, I spent many nights

with my Aunt Susan in Rhode Island, and
learned more about my mother's mother than
I had ever wanted to know. I also managed—
through my cousin Davy—to make friends off-
island, friends who believed I was like them.
And I had a lot of friends as a child.

Although I was not considered handsome
at first—at least not by my mother, who found
my hair to be too ominous in some way, my
eyes too blue and perhaps too sharp, my
manner arrogant (even as an eight-year-old,
she'd called me that)—I began learning the
secret of athletics early and applied myself to
molding my body the same way I went about
molding my mind. I studied and read and
found the boys who seemed to know what they
were doing, and I gravitated toward them. I
learned what they knew by nature. I was unco-
ordinated in most sports, until I realized that,
as in all things, it was about breathing.

This is one of the secrets of life:

It's all about breathing.

VOICES IN THE DARK:

"It's all right, I know you. I know what we
both want."

"Shut up. Just shut up."

"Come here. Come here. Let me help you. It's all right. It feels good."

"No, not like this. No."

"I've been so lonely."

"Oh."

"Wanting this."

"Oh."

"Since the first time I saw you."

"Oh."

HAVE you ever felt that you would do anything to be with someone?

I almost feel sorry for you, if you haven't.

THE PURITY of life is in the secrets—they're simple, they say everything, they are there for anyone, but we must wake up to the purity first in order to understand the secrets.

My pursuit of physical excellence began early. I tackled solitary athletics since this seemed best for my character. They were also cheaper. My family was poor—have I mentioned that? Not *poor* poor. Not "out in the street with no food" poor, but poor nonetheless.

My mother's first husband had been rich, but had also been a gambler. My mother—I should call her Boston, for that's what my father called her even though her name was Helen—had been the fifth daughter in a wealthy family who had married well, briefly, the first time around. But that man—someone I had never in my life heard of beyond knowing he existed—apparently lost all his and Helen's money, and soon she found my father, a good man (one would suppose) who ended up working as a gardener for rich folk. It paid well enough—like I said, we weren't *poor* poor.

My father probably would've had more money, but he had a sister who was dying—for years—down in Annapolis, Maryland, and he was her only support. So, according to my mother, half of his income went to her upkeep. "She has the longest-lived cancer I've ever heard of," she'd say, sometimes right in front of him.

Of course, this wasn't all there was to it, but if I tell you all the secrets of the world at once, you'll either be dazzled or overwhelmed, and there's no point in making it all explode right now. You'll want to know why breathing is one of the secrets of life.

You know how breathing is voluntary? I've

heard that people with dementia sometimes end up forgetting how to breathe. That's a terrible way to die, although one would suppose that any method of dying would be awful. Well, breathing is the essential component of accomplishing anything.

I observed this early—I was on the school bus, and I noticed a little girl next to me who was terrified of an upcoming test we were about to take. She would, in fact, stop breathing for seconds at a time. I began to count her breaths. I noticed that for every one breath I took, she took four. I suggested to her that she try just concentrating on her breathing.

After a bit of persuasion, she did.

It didn't seem to work.

I held up my father's watch —the one I'd stolen. (Yes, I stole things regularly around the house. I have reasons, none of which you want to know.) I had learned a bit about hypnosis, so I asked her to gaze at the brass back of the watch as it caught sunlight through the bus window.

She asked me if I'd be putting her under. I told her that was up to her. This was, after all, just suggestion, nothing more. I would propose something and hope her mind would accept it. Of course, I was a child. I didn't

say it that way. I said it in some little
boy way.

She stared at the watch so much her eyes
teared up.

I began to slow her breathing. By the time
we reached school, she wasn't upset about the
test beyond what might be considered a
normal concern.

I began asking the other boys—the older
ones who were good at softball and running—
about the secrets their success. To get them to
trust me, I entertained them with my modest
ventriloquism skills—I could do birdcalls and
the sounds of crickets and even get brief
sentences out without moving my lips.

Boys like entertainment, so they opened up
and told me about athletics and sports. They
all said screwy things, but what I noticed were
two solid answers:

Breathing and imagination.

They made sure that they breathed
through everything. They also imagined that
they would win. This was a huge revelation to
me, since I had never felt that I could win
anything. I realized that these other boys were
winners in athletics because they in fact
believed they were—whether from coaches,
friends, family or whomever—and because
they did not stop breathing. They used their

breathing—without even knowing it—to help keep their bodies working.

All right, that may sound simplistic. I believe that the simplest things can lead to the strongest results.

So, I began to work on breathing in a way I hadn't before.

This was not merely inhaling and exhaling, but swimming at the beach in the icy spring and holding my breath underwater. After all, if I were going to be lord of my own breath, I needed to master everything about it, didn't I? I wasn't sure that I'd ever be a great breath-holder, because I never seemed able to go much beyond a minute. I was holding on too much to my fear of dying.

This is one of the first lessons about breathing—if you have breath within your lungs, you will not die. Death comes once there is no more breath.

Again, simple.

Again, true.

"Owen," my mother said, pinning the laundry up outside the cottage that the Montgomerys housed us in. "What in god's name are you doing?"

I had come up after logging in a minute-and-a-half beneath the water, right at the rocky ledge. I had just leaned over and thrust my face underwater. I was eleven at the time. I tried to explain to her the principle behind my experiment, but she did not seem to understand.

However, within a few short months, I had become best friends with the captain of the swim team in seventh grade, and by fall, I was running cross-country. I would never be the best—this was not my goal, after all. I would be a winner. In fact, I knew I would close in on this with each sport or endeavor I tried, because the other kids were lazy. Life and their families made them that way. I did not intend to let a day go by which I could not claim for my own. I was going to own life in a way that neither of my parents ever had. Academics slipped in my middle-school years—but not enough for anyone to notice. I read studiously, and never for enjoyment, but to understand systems of thought that the world was trying to push at us.

I learned quickly that an A+ in school sometimes meant a D- in life, and that equal effort had to be made to excel in both spheres.

When I felt overwhelmed by it all, I practiced my breathing again. Swimming helped, too, when everything around me grew dark and terrible.

Even in December, when the island was

desolate and the water cold enough to freeze you to death, I might leap into the sea and stay beneath the water as long as I could stand it. Other icy days, I'd use the Montgomerys' indoor swimming pool for my morning workouts.

THAT WAS the wonderful thing about the Montgomerys' place: they were usually gone all winter unless Mr. and Mrs. Montgomery were fighting, or Mr. Montgomery had gone off with one of his mistresses and Mrs. M was so angry she came to the island for a blisteringly cold February. I used to see Mrs. M in those cold Februarys, and I ran errands in town for her because she spent too much time staring at the walls or sitting along the indoor pool while I did laps.

She enjoyed letting me swim there, and she sometimes even got in and did laps, too.

Once, when I was twelve, Mrs. M told me, "You're turning into quite the handsome boy, Owen Crites."

She was in good shape for a woman of forty, and there were times when I was with her that she reminded me so much of Jenna it was almost like having Jenna there with me.

When I watched her back, as she got out of the pool, bathing cap on, her narrow waist, the way the water beaded upon her skin—it was like seeing Jenna for a moment. This made me happy. Jenna meant a lot to me.

But the pool—dare I describe it now, how I remember it? It was vast. It was Olympic size. I could do real laps there, as opposed to laps at the beach which ended with a summer lifeguard blowing a whistle for me to come to shore before I'd gone out twenty yards. It was off the southern wing of their estate, surrounded with glass, so that it was as if you were swimming outside, as if on the bluffs over the Sound.

You owned the world as you went back and forth, carefully breathing so as not to wear out too fast.

During those winters when the Montgomerys stayed down in Manhattan, my father and mother and I had the run of the house. I could swim naked in the pool and rise to see the reflection of my body in the long mirrors in the small locker room off the pool. By sophomore year in high school I had created—and mastered—a beautiful, strong body. What average looks I had were masked by health and physical near-perfection.

I didn't admire this physique because I believed in beauty.

Beauty is for the lazy.

I admired it because I knew the world admired it. I wanted to own the world.

Wrestling was my winter sport at school, and I did not excel at it, but I held my own. The girls loved me—and the boys, too. I never got too close to them, because I had to spend all my energy creating who the person they wanted to see. The girls all cheered for me during sweaty matches when I brought some great bull of a boy from a competing school down hard to the red mat. Because the psychological aspect to sports can't be emphasized enough, I would—with each match—create some threat to my opponent. Something I could whisper in his ear. This took no small planning as it meant doing research on the boys I might wrestle so I'd know just what button to push to give me a psychological edge.

Dagon helped me. My god took me to books and ideas and *notions* that showed me just what other boys might be most hurt by. Usually, it involved their sense of sexuality.

After all, even *I* knew that showering with other boys, wearing jockstraps, cracking jokes about assorted vulgarities and nicknaming genitalia drew a thin veil across homoeroticism among adolescents.

And who but wrestlers were closest to puncturing that veil?

So, I'd whisper to my opponent something about him, something perhaps his closest friend had told me—his closest friend, drunk, being taken out to a parking lot—his closest friend who, with six beers in him, would finally admit to something that my opponent would be happiest to hide for a thousand years. Sometimes, it was less interesting.

My threat might be, "I know your little sister, Trey. I know all about her leg. I would hate for something to happen to her. I would hate for someone to do something to a little girl so sweet."

You may judge me for this if you like.

It was a competitive edge. This is what we, in athletics, were taught: *find your edge*. Skill alone never wins. I wish it did, but lazy people think that way. Faith is necessary, too. I had found mine. It had grown within me.

Now, my whisperings to opponents ignited rumors about me, but I'd built up a loyal enough following of other boys and girls in school. I became head of the pep squad for the football team—team sports were never my thing, but I knew that I had to somehow attach myself to them. So, when kids from other schools began talking about me saying "crazy, psycho" things, I had friends who were willing to lie down and die for me rather than accept those lies.

I really liked the kids I went to high school with; I liked the teachers. It was easy for me to like them. I think even being poor helped—teachers saw me as an underdog rising. I would tutor children in the local elementary school some afternoons; I took the coach's daughter to the junior prom, just because I was a nice guy and I felt bad that she wasn't pretty enough to get asked by any of the other guys. I was well-liked, and sometimes, that carries you.

But I haven't mentioned much about Jenna yet, have I? In all this talk of myself, she hasn't yet entered—not in the way she should have. She didn't go to my school. She barely existed within my sphere. She was *outer*, her world spun beyond the beyond. How could I even take her to the prom when she only arrived at Outerbridge Island in the summers?

I would count the days until Memorial Day weekend, when the Outerbridge Majesty would arrive in Quonnoquet Haven, heavy with tourists and summer people, and there, on the highest deck, I'd see her with my binoculars and then lie back in the muddy grass to look up at the pale sky and think: Please remember what we promised. Remember everything and don't leave anything out. Remember why I came to you and why you let me and why it would make everything be the way it was supposed to, and why you're the reason for my every breath.

That's what had happened when I was twelve and dedicated my soul to the god of dark places. By the time I was seventeen, I was a dedicated servant to the one I worshipped. And the only thing I asked of this divinity was:

Give me Jenna.

I'LL TELL you what really happened the summer I discovered purity—*genuine purity*—in the shit of human existence.

I can see myself as I was then, young, even pretty in a way with my thick hair falling to either side of my face, my eyes sharp, yes, but expectant. My polo shirt a preppie affectation —my mother never wanted me to look like the other islanders, she wanted something better for me, as did I. Khakis, no socks, catalog-ordered moccasins or village-made leather sandals—my face burning from the beginnings of summer sun, my heart racing.

It's no longer me as I am. It's that boy, this boy who is almost eighteen, maybe a man at this point, a boy who moves in the direction from "want" to "have."

I, he, you, it doesn't matter what I call that boy-man, he just exists in this globe of eternal summer. I can feel his breath and smell dime-store cologne on him. When he smiles I can see the cap on his front tooth that cost his father a pretty penny after he fell and chipped it in sixth grade while running.

I sense a dense fog lifting between this day and that one.

He watches, this magnificent Owen Crites, for her.

A WINDOW VIEW

Owen Crites looked to summer for one thing, and one thing only. It would be the arrival of Jenna Montgomery, and that would mean his misery, his feelings of loneliness would vanish. He could nearly forget himself.

Where is she? he wondered, remembering the first time he knew she belonged with him.

"Hɪ," he said to her when they were both six.

"Hi," she replied. But she hadn't needed to. She was all ringlets and ribbons and party dress.

"Owen," he said.

"I know. Hank's your daddy."

The fact that she called his father by his first name shocked Owen. No other child called a parent by the first name. It was taboo. And to call his father "Hank" and not "Henry" seemed far too familiar.

"I know where you live," she added, an afterthought.

"Down the hill," he said.

"In my yard," she said. "You're near my goldfish pond."

"Koi," he corrected her.

"And all the roses my mommy loves," she said, and then took him by the hand and brought him into her world—the birthday party, the beautiful children from New York, the pony rides on the bluffs, the smoked turkey sandwiches, the games of pin-the-tail, and the dance.

He had been woefully underdressed in a torn pair of jeans and a T-shirt. The other boys all wore white shirts and little ties; their hair glistened with gel. The girls were in puffy dresses and glittery shoes. He had no gift for her then. It had panicked him midway through the party.

Owen took a gift off the pile from among those she hadn't yet opened. He threw away the other child's card. On the wrapping paper, he scrawled "*Happy Birthday from Owen.*"

As it turned out, the gift was a small hand puppet, and Owen took it from Jenna and began doing something that he didn't even know he could do. He threw his voice, so it sounded as if the puppet was speaking without Owen's lips moving. Even Mrs. M commented to Owen's mother about her son's delightful talent.

Owen received punishment for presenting the gift as his own, but he didn't mind.

Punishment was the result of knowledge. Smart people punished themselves, his older self knew. All people with brains received punishment.

From then on, Jenna Montgomery became everything to him. In all those years from child to boy to man, he never experienced a night without thinking of her.

His teenage years nearly past, Owen waited for her, watching the glinting sea for the ferry on the Thursday before Memorial Day weekend.

HIS EYES TURNED to slits against the western sun; it was the last ferry of the day, and he couldn't find her or her parents among those on the deck.

Perhaps she wouldn't be coming until after the holiday—it had happened before. He didn't want to believe it because he never liked to consider the options that people had. His own life felt without options. He had created within himself the person who could most handle his life. He had worked his body, developed the grace of an athlete, he had tried to keep his face pleasant—and when the anxieties of his family or of studies became unbearable, he would go to the mirror and practice relaxing his facial features until he was sure he looked pleasant again. He did not want to seem anxious, even if he was. He wanted to give nothing away to those around him.

He ran down to the docks to see if she might be somewhere else on the ferry— perhaps she was sick and wanted to stay below. Perhaps she was taking a nap in the back seat of her family's Range Rover. Perhaps, perhaps, he repeated to himself as he sloughed off inertia, and jogged down to the paved road near the marina.

The summer people were like ticks—they attached themselves to every aspect of the island, they drank all the beer, they ate the best the local cooks had to offer, they had all the accidents—more people would die from boating or swimming mishaps in three months than would die in six years during other seasons.

They were careless, they were bloodsucking, they were here to forget the venal world from which they came. They, he thought. *They.* They debarked the ferry, bicyclists, clownish men and women in golfing outfits, or overly gilded women with poodles and wolfhounds and shih tzus, followed by weary overworked doctor-husbands; the college crowd, too, had begun filling up the local bars and the beach, and all these he hated with a passion. He had spent his life watching them come and be carefree in the summer.

He had watched them spend more money some nights than his father could make in a month.

Dagon, he prayed, Dagon, hear me. Cast them down. Raise me up.

He ached for what they had. The lives they possessed. The freedom from this island. From the world he had mastered.

He read books on Manhattan; he learned about Jenna's family, how her great-great-grandfather had worked on railroads and then had gone on to own them, and how her great-grandfather had lost that fortune; how her grandfather had gotten into radio and television and magazines, owning several, selling them, building up a small but substantial media empire; how her mother had continued that work, married a great media magnate, divorced, married again, had Jenna and remained with Mr. M although the marriage ran hot and cold.

The story of Jenna's family was the story of all the summer people, and though they lived simply on the island for the three months, though they rode cheap bikes around the Great Salt Pond, though they dressed casually even for the one restaurant in Old Town Harbor (the Salty Dog), they were all over-moneyed as his father often said.

His father spoke of money as evil; his mother spoke of it as if it were a lost child.

Owen felt money was something like fire—to be feared and mastered. It was what other people were given. It was what he would be granted. And these people tromping off the ferry had it. They lived it. They did not dream of getting off this island. They dreamed of things beyond what Owen could imagine.

JENNA DIDN'T ARRIVE at the harbor that day. He walked the long, narrow wooden staircase from the beach up to the bluffs, and ran along the fringe of pines to the dirt path that went further up the rolling cliffs. He didn't look back down to the water until he was at their property.

At the house, he went and sat in one of the wrought-iron lawn chairs and leaned back to gaze up at the sky.

"Owen?"

He sat up, looking around. He rose from the chair, practically knocking it over, and there she was—at the third-story attic window.

No, it was Mrs. M. Her auburn hair was swept back from her face, damp from the swimming pool; her robe fastened none too tight.

"Owen? It's good to see you."

"Yeah, Mrs. M, me too. I didn't think you had got here just yet."

"Oh, my husband still hasn't left his desk yet. I've been here since Wednesday. Good to be back. I despise the city."

"Survive winter okay?"

"Superbly," she said, but in a way that meant its opposite. Mrs. M was a woman full of irony; he had known it for years. Mrs. M. embodied the house: beautiful, classic, and rich.

"Do you want coffee?" she asked.

"I SAW YOU WAITING FOR HER," Mrs. M said.

They were in the sunroom off the kitchen. Owen had just finished his first cup of cinnamon coffee. He got up to pour himself another, but Mrs. M interceded. She had a fresh cup, with cream, all ready for him. He sat down at the table again.

She took the chair across from him. He saw her knee emerge from her robe. The hint of breast, like a reward.

Mrs. M was in many ways more beautiful than her daughter; but still, his heart belonged to Jenna.

He did what he could to look at her face, but something in her eyes bothered him. He looked, instead, at her silken arms.

"You're in love with my daughter. No, that's fine. I've known it since you were both young. Do you think it will lead anywhere?"

"Lead?" He said the word innocently, but she must've seen through him. "I don't know."

"Yes, you do. You're smart. But, do you think she's right for you?"

"I haven't…I haven't considered…" he stammered.

"You're a remarkable young man," Mrs. M said. "She doesn't deserve you."

Then, she put down her own untouched coffee and got up, drawing her robe together. "She gets in tonight. After midnight."

"How? The ferry—"

"She has her ways," Mrs. M said. She brushed something from the edge of her eye and combed her hands through her hair like a mermaid would. "Fancy a swim?"

"Not today," he said.

"Come on, just a nice long swim. Haven't you been practicing all winter?"

He nodded.

"I thought so. You ripple now. You don't move, you ripple. You're in better shape than he is," Mrs. M said, and then went to get her bathing suit.

COME MIDNIGHT, he saw the shroud of a blue and white sailboat press beneath the lights of the harbor. He sat up on the bluffs and watched as she docked; the sail came down. No one stepped off the boat at the jetty. Was it her? Was this what Mrs. M had meant?

He fell asleep in the cool wet grass and awoke at dawn.

And he knew.

Jenna Montgomery had found another.

In the afternoon, at the Montgomerys', Owen met his rival.

"Jimmy," the guy said, his face gleaming, tanned, teeth so thoroughbred he could've raced in Saratoga, his eyes squinty, his nose small, his hair honey-blond from too much sun, and his handshake strong and sure and arrogant. He looked rich without ever having to say it. He smelled rich. He probably tasted rich.

"Good to meet you, Crites."

"Owen."

"You're not an Owen or a Crites," Jimmy said. "You're a Mooncalf."

"Mooncalf?" Jenna laughed, looking at Owen and then back at Jimmy. "That sounds ghastly."

She wore a bikini, but had a long towel draped about her waist that ran all the way to her ankles. Her hair was wet and shining from a morning swim.

For a moment, Owen imagined how it would feel to untie the bikini top and press his face against her breasts. For a moment, the image was in his mind; then, gone.

All Owen could think was: they'd slept together on the boat. Jenna and this Jimmy character. Jimmy had done it with Jenna. Done it. A sacred act if it was love. A debased ritual, if it was lust and emptiness. Which it had to be. He tried not to imagine Jimmy drawing her legs apart, or the scent of passion that clung to them, the sweat and fever, as they joined together. Tried not to imagine the thrusts.

"Mooncalf reminds me of upstate New York, or Pennsylvania," Jenna said with no little disgust. "Cows and chickens. Amish in carriages. Birthings and midwives. Owen can't be a Mooncalf."

Jim snorted. "No, it's a beautiful name. Mooncalf."

Owen remained silent, still numb from meeting the interloper.

"Well, if he's a Mooncalf then what am I?"

"Kitten." Jimmy laughed.

"If I'm Kitten, then you're Cat."

"All right, then I'm Cat. Now, what shall we call this island?"

"Outerbridge," Owen said. "Call it Outerbridge."

"That's not the game." Jimmy grinned, and damn if his smile wasn't dazzling. Anyone would fall in love with this guy, anyone, man, woman, or dog, he was so damn attractive and warm, it made Owen want to walk away and forget about Jenna completely. "The game is everything, Mooncalf. It doesn't matter what things are. You shape them into the way you want them. That's how you gain mastery."

"Mastery's the thing," Owen said, faking a sort of blissful—and very nearly nonchalant—take on all of it. I'll beat you, he thought as he watched his rival, this Apollonian boy with his golden hair and squinty green eyes; his arrogance felt absolutely seductive.

I will beat you, Owen made the oath then and there.

He glanced briefly up at the unfettered sun and prayed to God that if nothing else went his way in this life, he would beat down this Jimmy.

Then, Owen reached a hand out and gave Jimmy's shoulder a friendly squeeze. "Just not big on games, I guess."

Jenna laughed. "Owen, the game is called Paradise. You rename everything to your liking. Jimmy invented it. Isn't it…marvelous?"

She pecked the bastard on his ear.

Owen noted: the kiss went to his earlobe, and Jimmy barely had an earlobe. His ear was smooth and rounded and touched down right behind one of his several dimples.

Jimmy laughed, shrugging, grabbing her around the waist and pulling her close to him.

"Let's call the island Sea Biscuit."

"No," Jenna groaned. "That's terrible. Terrible. Owen, you name it."

"Outerbridge," Owen said.

It was noon, and they were at the jetty. The sailboat bobbed gently with the current, and Owen finally took his baseball cap off.

"There now," Jimmy said, approvingly. "You look less like a little boy and more like a man. The Mooncalf has such pretty hair for a moody guy."

He reached over and scruffed his hand through Owen's hair. His fingers felt electric.

"I know the name for this island. I know. It's called Bermuda. We're in Bermuda." He laughed, leaning into Jenna, kissing her just behind her ear.

No, Owen thought.

You're in the realm of Dagon.

A RESTLESS NIGHT came to him, and then another and another. He lay on his single bed, sheets pulled back, and a fever such as he had never before felt washed over him.

Whosoever has loved the way I love Jenna

Montgomery, he whispered to the stars through his bedroom window, has known sacrifice and torture and days and nights of endless wanting, thirst without satisfaction, hunger without morsel. Whosoever has wept within themselves for what they could not reach, could not touch, has felt what I feel.

Whosoever has spent his life working his body, mind, and soul to its absolute limit to become the extreme candidate for the love of a beautiful and angelic girl as I have for her, as I have given myself to the shape that she would long for…

That man would not rest were a rival to steal the prize from him.

Dagon, he whispered soundlessly. *Dagon. My god. Bring her to me.*

Eventually, Owen Crites slept better imagining the world under the sea where the people who were part of the Dagon realm dwelt, with their vast and imperious citadels, their large cold eyes and wet shapeless forms. He imagined the great sacrifice he would throw to them for their entertainment.

"HOW ARE you going to waste your last summer?" Owen's mother asked as she switched off the faucet, plunging her hands back into the soapy water. "Now, don't blot, Owen, dry. There's a difference."

She passed him the first dish, which he sprayed down and then wiped with the green-and-white hand towel. The kitchen in the caretaker's house was as narrow as one of the closets in the big house; but the window looked out on a small sunken garden, behind which the pine trees stuck out like crooked teeth.

"Don't blot," his mother repeated.

Owen began stacking the dry plates carefully.

"I need a job."

"You work for your father."

"Not this summer," he replied. "Hank'll do without me."

"Hank?" his mother said, nearly laughing. "Hank? Next you'll be calling me Trudy." Then, her mood darkened. "Show some respect."

His mother reached down to pull the plug on the drain. She reached back to her hairpins, pulling them out so that her gray-streaked hair fell along her shoulders. She smoothed it back, and turned to watch him dry the rest of the plates and bowls from supper. "I know what you're thinking."

He glanced at her for the barest moment.

"You're thinking that you'll work down where she goes at night. The restaurant. The dock. You'll be there for the dances. I've seen the boys working at those places. They live here all year round. But in the summer, sometimes they get the rich girls. But those girls don't care about them. The boys are just part of summer to those girls. Just like the beach. Just like a walk."

He remained silent, and kept his eyes on each bowl as he carefully wiped the towel through them.

"I grew up in her world. I know what she'd have to give up. Don't ask her to do it. Not if you care about her," his mother said.

Then, she nearly snickered.

"What's funny?" he asked.

"I remember your father when he wasn't much older than you. I remember him so well," she said. "He had big dreams. He's working on the pump now. The pump and the well. Today he worked on the azaleas and the rosebushes. Tomorrow, he'll probably check the pool. If I had only known. Owen, you might as well go find that pirate treasure as think a girl like that will be interested in you beyond a summer fling."

Owen dropped the towel on top of the cutting board, and turned to walk away.

"I know what you get up to," his mother called to him, but he had already stepped out of the house, letting the screen door swing lazily shut. "You're nearly a man, Owen. You need to grow out of all your imaginings now."

Her voice, behind him, was part of another layer of existence. The smell of fresh grass mingled with the slight scent of the roses which were just blooming in spirals and curves up on the bluffs. He walked to the edge of the hill, feeling the late sun stroke him like a warm hand.

At the rim of the koi pond, he knelt down and looked at his reflection in the green water. Soon, the patchwork fish came to the surface. He reached his hand into the murkiness, shivering with the chill, and found the god lying where he'd left it, behind the lava rocks.

He felt the edge of the god's face.

IN A SCHOOL NOTEBOOK, Owen wrote:

Things Jenna likes.

1. She loves swing dancing.

2. She likes expensive perfume. The kind older women wear. Not like other girls.

3. She likes sandals.

4. She likes to let a boy open a door for her.

5. She likes clothes from Manhattan.

6. She likes to be complimented on how smart she is.

7. She likes someone who listens to her.

8. She likes holding hands.

Things Jenna hates:

1. She hates heavy metal rock.

2. She hates boys who look at her breasts.

3. She hates having to wait for anything. Ever.

4. She hates most movies. She reminds me of movie stars though.

5. She hates when animals get hurt.

6. She hates being treated like a piece of meat.

7. She hates boys who want to go all the way because she told me three years ago that she's going to wait for the right one.

8. She hates having to do things she hates.

HE WAITED a week before going back up to the Montgomery place, and even then, it was after eleven, and the house was dark and silent except for the kitchen, where Mrs. M always kept a light on.

At first, he intended to stand beneath

Jenna's bedroom window and maybe toss a pebble at it to get her attention.

He noticed that the window—on the third story—was open, and he decided he'd call to her.

Then, he noticed that one of the guest room windows was open, too.

That would be Jimmy's.

The bastard.

Owen glanced along the trellis and gutters, and decided he'd try that route first. He climbed the trellis with the agility of a monkey, although it threatened to pull away if he didn't balance his weight just right. It wasn't much different from the rope climb in gym.

When he worried that he wouldn't make it to the third-story roof, he remembered the breathing trick and began inhaling and exhaling carefully. That was where the balance was: in the breathing.

Then, he grabbed the rain gutter, and scaled the slant of the roof. He crawled along it, slowly, cautiously, and went to look in on Jenna while she slept.

He felt himself grow hard, imagining how he could hold her while she slept, imagining how he would smell her hair.

When he looked through the open window, he saw the other boy there, Jimmy, in bed with her, holding her, moving against her. Owen caught his breath and held it for what felt like the longest time.

He could hold his breath underwater for a few minutes. He held it while watching Jimmy press himself into her like a hummingbird jabbing at a flower but not as pretty. Just dark and murky with Jimmy's body rising and falling as he plunged, not gently the way she would want it, but like a jackal tearing apart some carcass.

A MORNING SWIM

"*he Salty Dog,*" Owen said, lifting himself from the swimming pool. "Waiting tables. Since Memorial Day weekend. Lifting weights, too."

"That must be delightful," Mrs. M said.

She stood near the changing rooms, swathed in a sheer robe beneath which her green bathing suit shimmered, dark glasses covering her eyes. She looked like a movie star. She had a cigarette in her hand, which she waved dramatically.

"I imagine you meet lots of others your age at that dive."

"Some."

"You're still very young," she said, and then caught her breath for a moment. "I'm sorry. I didn't mean that in a negative way. I meant it as…as…you're so innocent compared to the boys at that school Jenna goes to. They've already begun those patterns they'll have for life."

She exhaled a lungful of smoke. *She's like a beautiful dragon*, he thought. *A jade dragon with sparkling eyes.*

Owen drew himself up over the pool's edge. He exhaled deeply, coughing.

"My smoking bother you?"

"No," he said, swiveling to sit down more comfortably, his legs still in the water. "Just holding my breath. Trying, anyway."

"Trying to reach some goal? Underwater?" She took her sunglasses off, and dropped them carelessly on the tiles.

He nodded. "To beat the *Guinness Book of World Records*. This guy, he held his breath. Thirteen minutes."

"That's impossible." She walked casually over to him. He could see her sapphire bathing suit top, and her breasts cupped within it as her robe fell open. She stepped out of her sandals.

For a moment, he imagined what she would look like with her suit ripped from chin to thigh, with him pressing into her— no, not him, Jimmy, the way he had torn into Jenna.

Mrs. M, a smile on her face, could not read his thoughts, he hoped.

"No one can hold his breath that long," she said. "It must've been a cheat."

"If you believe in something, maybe you can do impossible stuff, Mrs. M."

"That's magical thinking, sweetie. And Mrs. M, good lord." She laughed, dropping her robe completely. She shimmered. "You're a man now. You'll have to start calling people by their first names, Owen. I feel like a schoolmarm when you call me that. Is that what you want me to feel like? A haggish old schoolmarm? I'm forty, not seventy. Catherine. Or Cathy."

"Oh, yeah, okay," he said, grinning. "Cathy."

As she walked along the edge of the pool to the far end, she pulled her hair back and tucked it into her white bathing cap. She lifted her arm in a certain way to him, like a salute. Then, she dove into the pool, graceful as a mermaid.

He watched her do laps while he caught his breath.

W HEN HE WENT to shower off, Owen saw the

other boy's towel hanging from the bathroom stall.

Steam began to fill the changing room. Owen pulled his wet trunks down, and tossed them on a chair. He grabbed one of the long white towels that the Montgomerys' maid kept neatly rolled in the cabinet over the toilet. Then, he walked the narrow hallway to the large shower.

All three shower heads were running, and Jimmy stood there rubbing soap along his arms, his face frothy with white soap foam.

Owen ignored him, and—stepping beneath the spray—grabbed a bar of soap from the shelf.

"Mooncalf," Jimmy said, as the foam rinsed from his face. His hair stuck up high on his head. The smell of soap was overpowering. "Haven't seen you in a while."

"I know," Owen said, his voice husky.

He didn't feel the way he did in school with the other boys, not with this Jimmy, this eighteen-year-old who he had watched deflower Jenna. He felt disgusted.

"Been busy."

He turned his back on Jimmy for the rest of the shower, hoping the other boy would leave to go swim in the pool. But Jimmy toweled off, and began dressing just as Owen turned off the water. He slipped his shorts on, and reached for his T-shirt.

"You've been working out a lot. Me, too. I run every morning. I play tennis."

"Swim," Owen said. He walked back to the toilet to take a leak.

"Swim?"

"I swim."

"Ah, a complete sentence out of the Mooncalf." Jimmy chuckled. "That's the first thing I noticed about you, you know."

Owen said nothing; flushed the toilet. Sat down on one of the chairs, and reached for his shirt.

"You talk in bits of sentences. Well, that and your hair."

Owen twisted back to look at him, his T-shirt half over his head.

"My hair?"

"You've got pretty hair. It's soft, too. Most guys' hair is like bristles."

"Weirdo," Owen said. "Sleep in any of the guest rooms much?"

He pulled the shirt down, and then went to grab his socks. Jimmy followed him, sitting across on a short bench.

"I don't even know what the guest rooms look like. I sleep with Jenna. That bother you?"

"No. It's weird her parents don't care."

"Her mother doesn't. Her father's still down in the city. And anyway," he said, shrugging, "you seem to know a lot about where I sleep. I'm hoping you don't sneak around and look through windows or anything."

Owen averted his eyes, glancing down at his feet.

"Hope it doesn't bother you, Mooncalf," Jimmy said. "When we first met, I thought you might be hot for Jenna."

"We're friends. That's all."

"Boys can't just be friends with girls. We always want something else."

"Okay," Owen said. He laughed, but it was fake. It echoed off the turquoise tile and sounded less genuine as it went. He looked at Jimmy, who was watching him the way Owen's father would when trying to figure him out.

"You know, Mooncalf, you comb your hair to the left a little more—make the part slightly higher—and you'd look top drawer. You really would. Your chin's strong, your body's fit. You need to get rid of these," Jimmy pointed at Owen's T-shirt, "and start wearing some oxford cloths, button-downs. With sleeves. Short sleeves are for kids. It would show your best side. And maybe some khakis. When you grin, don't show all your teeth."

"Bite me."

Jimmy laughed and reached out, pressing his hand against Owen's shoulder in what could only be a casual and friendly—even brotherly—gesture.

"Good. Some spirit. I'm just trying to help. You look good, but you look too island. You need a little charm. All guys do. Swimming only goes so far, after all." Jimmy, ever annoying, kept up the jabber. "I'm not much of a swimmer. I sail, but the idea of water, well, let's just say I do a passable dog paddle. But you've got those biceps. Amazing shoulders for such a Mooncalf runt. Pretty good. How much you bench?"

"Who cares?"

A brief silence.

Then, "I do."

"Well, not all that much," Owen said. "I just stack the weights on and push. I don't notice how much."

"Don't notice? My god, sport, you mean to say your goal isn't the weights?"

Owen shrugged. "I never think about it. I just want to be powerful. I mean strong."

"You said powerful."

"Same thing."

Another brief silence.

"You ever up for tennis?" Jimmy asked.

"Not really."

"I can teach you if you like. It'd be fun to a doubles match one day. Early, before it's too hot. You, me, Jenna, and maybe you could find a friend to bring. It's always fun to play doubles," Jimmy said.

Owen noticed the combination of arrogance and nonchalance, as if none of this mattered.

Jimmy probably screwed Jenna on a nightly basis. But he never thought about Owen, or Owen and Jenna. He probably lived in the moment. Completely.

"Saturday should be a ton of fun," Jimmy said, wiping the last of the spray from his shoulders as he pushed his feet into the cheapest sneakers that Owen had ever seen. "You bringing a date?"

Owen glanced up. "Her birthday?"

"Yeah, you know, the whole crowd's coming from the Cape, and then we'll just do tequila shots till dawn. You got a girl off-island?"

Owen began to lie, just to fill that emptiness between them. Yes, he had a girl. Yes, he was excited about Jenna's birthday party, even though he had not been invited to it. Yes, he was considering his options as to which colleges he was looking into—Middlebury looked promising, he didn't think he had quite the grades for Harvard, but his uncle had been a dean at Middlebury, and yes, they could all go skiing in the winter up there on some distant holiday.

The whole time Owen was talking, Jimmy reached into his shaving kit. He went over to shave at the mirror and applied some kind of lotion to his face. He finished it off with a spritz of the most obnoxious cologne that Owen had ever smelled. While they small-talked it, Owen knew, standing there in the diminishing steam of the changing room, he *knew*.

Just by standing there with Jimmy in the shimmering mist.

Jimmy had a weakness.

Owen began spending a lot of time, after that, thinking about that weakness.

Thinking about how he could get Jenna back.

OWEN'S SHIFT at the Salty Dog began at three and lasted until eleven, six days a week. He emerged sweaty and stinking of grease, because half his job was cleaning out the fryers and grease pits at the end of the night, and when he got off shift in early July—it was nearly two a.m.—he went down to the jetty to stare out at the early morning mist of the Sound, smoke some cigarettes, and chill.

He didn't turn around when he heard the footsteps coming up behind him.

"Mooncalf."

"Hey Jimmy."

"Got a cig?"

"Take one." Owen tossed a cigarette back.

"Thanks. I guess you want to be alone."

"Didn't know you smoked."

"I don't. Not when anyone looks, anyway."

"That's nice. Anything else you do when no one's looking?"

"If I told, you'd know my secrets."

"How's Jenna?"

"She's okay. She fell asleep early. I just needed to wander a little. How's the job?"

"Good. You can smell it on me. You wander late. It's almost morning."

"In Manhattan, I wander at all hours. I like this time of night. You meet all kinds of interesting people. I kind of miss work. I used to work summers in one of my dad's stores. It was fun sometimes."

"Seems like more fun to run around the island all summer. Like you two."

"It gets old. I take that back. Yeah, it's fun. I guess you want to be left alone."

"You guessed right," Owen said, cricking his neck to the left a bit.

"Your neck hurt?"

"It gets stiff. Leaning over a mop half the time. On my knees cleaning out all kinds of shit."

"Here," Jimmy said, and Owen felt hands at the back of his neck, gently massaging. "Better?"

Owen let him continue. "This fog depresses me."

"I think it's peaceful."

"You would."

"Mooncalf, you hate me, don't you?"

"Not really."

"How does this feel?" Jimmy pressed his thumbs into Owen's shoulders.

"Oh yeah," Owen said. "Right there."

BEFORE DAWN, he had gone to the pond. He knelt beside it, and reached down among the algae and slimy rocks until he found it.

He drew the statue up, and set it down on the wet grass.

"I guess you're just made up," he said

aloud. "I guess I'm just a screwed-up guy who made you up. Maybe when I was twelve I was warped. But you're just some cheap souvenir someone lost. No one believes in gods."

Still, the itchy thought touched him some-where between his eyes and scalp—he could practically feel the fire crawling on him.

But if you're not.

If you're real.

I'll do what needs to be done.

MRS. M, in her own words:

Here's what I thought of it all: my daughter Jenna had been trouble from the day she was born. She was pretty and plain at the same time, and I say that as a loving mother. She inherited her father's face, not much of mine, although I guess she got my eyes.

Lucky her—my least favorite feature, since my own mother always told me I had sad eyes. When Jenna was four years old, she told me that no man was going to do to her what her daddy did to me. Definitely wise beyond her years, but just not special enough to handle what life would deliver to her, that's for damn sure.

It was her trust fund. It made her trouble.

Look, there's something that everyone pussy-foots around but no one ever talks about. That's money. Pure and simple.

Money.

When a girl has some, she can be elevated to the status of goddess.

The most ordinary—even homely—creature can become ravishing with just a portfolio or a trust fund.

That island—in summer—is full of trust fund widows who should by all rights be considered blemishes, but instead are constantly sought out for parties and gatherings and literary events.

For Jenna, there's always been money. And I've watched it feed her in a way that can't be healthy; but what could I do? She has access to money. Lots of money. Money clothes her. She was ruined because of it, basically.

She could never learn how to survive. She could never learn how to rely on herself and her own character to get through a challenging situation. She could always buy her way out of things.

This isn't true of me. I was raised solidly middle-class. My father had died when I was six, and my mother didn't have too many options, not back then.

In many ways, I feel for Owen because of

that. Who wouldn't? His life is a lot like mine was as a child. Yes, there was some inheritance later for me, but when you spend most of your childhood wanting things you never really get over it.

And money becomes a prison, too. When you know what it's like to live without it, and when it's within your grasp, then you know what it's like to not have it.

So, you cling to it. Pure and simple. You hang on for dear life.

I suppose people will say things about my marriage to Frank that reflect this, but my marriage is a different kettle of fish. We've got our way of living, and yes, you can criticize it all you want, but it works for us nine times out of ten. Those times when it doesn't quite work, well, we have places to go where he can live his life and I can live mine, and the breather is well-needed. On both our parts.

I'm not the easiest woman in the world to live with. And he's no saint.

I sat down with my little girl when she was just learning about sex, and I told her that men have different ways of dealing with love, and usually it's through the one part of their body that seems to cause others the most damage.

"But it's just his body," I told her.

She cried over all of this. She cried when she found out her father had another woman. A mistress.

But you have to cry at first, don't you?

To get all those little fairy tales out of your head about how life gets lived, about how there are a few good men, how some men don't cheat. And it's not true.

All men cheat, and all women marry cheaters, and to not look at that square in the face is like not looking at the good side of marriage, too.

So she cried off and on for a few years, and I held her sometimes; I was cold to her at times—I knew she needed to work this idea out in her mind.

When she fell in love for the first time, she told me she was grateful for what she'd had to go through with her father.

"I don't know why men do what they do," she told me.

"If you did, you'd have solved the greatest mystery of life," I said to her. Or something like that.

But for my money, she should've avoided that Jimmy McTeague. He was bad news. I know every little deb and sorority girl east of the Mississippi thought he was just the end of the world, but they were such goofy little virgins it was hard to have patience with them.

Jimmy McTeague is the devil incarnate. I know that's an over-the-top way of putting it. He wasn't evil, but he was cold. I knew a little about his family, and none of it was very good. His father had some bad business deals going, and even if he had all the stores, Frank told me some things that alarmed me.

With Jimmy, I felt it the first day I met him, which was sometime before summer. Perhaps Easter break?

She brought him by the house in Greenwich, and the first thing out of his mouth was, "Hello, Catherine. I've heard so much about you, I almost feel like we've had an affair."

He thought that kind of thing was funny, that off-the-cuff jokiness. Within minutes, he'd given me some nickname, which of course he had to repeat five or ten times to truly annoy me, and within an hour of chatting with him, I knew more about that boy than I cared to know.

He is dangerous.

And so yes, I think it all has more to do with Jimmy McTeague than with anybody.

At her birthday party in late July, he told me that he thought the world was meant to be owned by people like him.

I believe those were his exact words.

Yes, he had money.

Yes, he was extremely good-looking for a boy his age. Extremely. Only a fool wouldn't notice that.

But he had no spirit. What he had was pure badness. He was absolutely pure in his badness.

I once had a dog like that. Beautiful. Completely bad. Jimmy McTeague's like that. I really began to hate that boy at Jenna's birthday party.

A BIRTHDAY PARTY

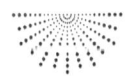

In the mirror, Owen combed his hair, parting it and fluffing it, not to the middle of his forehead, but certainly an inch above his usual. He also brushed it back so it rose even higher. The summer blond streaks looked better this way. He rubbed some gel into it, and made sure the part was clean.

He smiled as naturally as he could. No, that wasn't right. He let his lips pull back slightly. He squinted his eyes the way that Jimmy did. It looked rich to do it. Like the sun was always on his face, even on a cloudy day.

Then, he rubbed some of his mother's lotion on his face. It brought a shine to his cheeks and nose. He wasn't sure if he liked it, but it seemed to be what the rich boys had: that shine.

Hanging on the bathroom door: the crisp J.Crew shirt, pale blue, the tan chinos.

He dressed, and then returned to his bedroom to get the gift he'd wrapped that morning.

"You're not going to that party," his mother said, glancing at his father. Both sat in the small living room in the dark, the television providing the only source of light. Their faces flickered.

His father laughed. "Oh, he'll have fun. The kids are really going to mix it up."

"Yeah. It'll be fun."

"You're not one of them," his mother said. "You can pretend. You always pretend."

Then, she turned to his father, patting his shoulder. "Well?"

"Leave it alone, Boston," his father said. "It's the kid's party. You used to go to parties."

"What's that you've got there?" his mother asked. She got up from the couch, setting her beer down on the coffee table. His father reached over, turning on the standing lamp. Light came up. His mother looked gray despite the fact that she colored her hair. Even her skin seemed gray. His father looked like a wisp of smoke. It was all Owen could do to keep them from vanishing within the room.

Owen looked down at the box in his hands.

"It's her birthday."

"You bought her something?" his mother asked, a grin spreading like blood on her face.

He could imagine her dead, her skull cracked open like an egg.

"You bought the Montgomery girl something? Working for tips at the Salty Dog, and you bought the richest girl in the world something?" She shook her head gently. "Owen, you're always trying to impress someone with what you don't have." She said this sweetly.

He almost felt bad for what he'd done. He almost felt bad for what he'd stolen from his mother to put in the box.

He almost felt bad for what he was giving Jenna.

Almost.

THE PARTY WAS in full swing by ten at night. Every Nancy, every Skip, every Jess and Sloan —all were there, poolside.

The great curtains were drawn back, and the glass doors had been removed for the party. White tents had been erected along the yard; lanterns of every conceivable hue were strung along the walkway to the Montgomery place, and balloons flew with some regularity from the backyard. The smell of cigarettes and perfume and gin and beer and money were there, too.

Watching it, you'd have seen nearly fifty teenagers dancing, laughing, shouting, a tall blonde girl with flowing hair and limbs soaked from having been thrown into the swimming pool, the fat drunk frat boy vomiting over by the birdbath, half a dozen homely young women shining under the spotlight of boys' gazes—for lust and money and breeding and privilege all attract beyond mere looks.

The Sound sparkled with moonlight, and summer was at its peak; the sun had only just gone down an hour before, and the smell of salt sea air mingled with the foam of mermaids' souls, lost from true love.

All these things Owen thought.

"DID you see Jimmy at the nationals? God, I hear he's going to be at Wimbledon someday. Soon."

"If he's at Harvard—"

"When he's at Harvard, I'm going to call

him Jimmy McTeague of the Ivy League. Isn't that cute?"

"I think what's cute is his father. Have you ever met him?"

"Well, I've been in the store."

"Sports superstores never interested me. It seems crass to sell that kind of thing."

"I read in Forbes that his dad is worth several billion."

"Dead or alive?"

"Dead; then Jimmy's worth that."

"Jimmy McTeague is shallow. He is. He's not smart either," one deb said, her party dress ruined because someone spilled a Bloody Mary down the front. "He's pretty but he's dumb. And my uncle went to Yale with his father, and let me tell you, that man was nearly kicked out for cheating and once that kind of thing happens, you never know."

Owen stood back, beyond the lights that had been set up along the tents, and watched them all.

The small gift in its box, in his trembling hands.

"Smooth. Just be smooth," he whispered to himself.

He wanted to make sure Jenna saw the gift. Saw what it meant.

JIMMY MCTEAGUE HELD onto a bourbon and water as if for dear life, laughed with his jock friends, eyed the other girls but mainly when they were with their boyfriends, and he thanked Mrs. Montgomery for the excellent whiskey.

"People who have whiskey like this should own the world," and even as he said it, he didn't know what it meant.

When he saw Owen standing just at the edge of the party, he raised his glass and shouted, "Yo, Mooncalf, get your ass over here!"

JENNA MONTGOMERY, in her own words:

Here are things I've read somewhere or heard about and I really believe: The happiest people don't necessarily have the best of everything; they just make the most of everything that comes their way. Happiness only happens for those who have something to lose and cry over and those who get hurt, for only then can they can really appreciate things.

And maybe they deserve all the good things, too.

I think that, anyway.

Okay, before you think I'm just some rich bitch who gets sentimental and gooey over greeting cards and romance novels, the reason I think about those things is because when you are beautiful and you have money, it's those simple things you have to remember.

And I was pretty happy for the most part, right up until summer. But it's not like I never had sad things happen. Or didn't cry. Or didn't feel pain. That's all on the inside. You don't show it because people don't like people who cry over things.

This whole summer issue probably began because Daddy didn't want me to open Montgomery Hill on Memorial Day like we always did. Mom was already up there, a week or two early, and I'd only just come home from finals.

I have gone to Outerbridge Island since I was about four, and I never miss a summer there. It's what I look forward to after a tough year in school, and since I would turn eighteen over the summer and I had just finished school —but I'd be entering college in September—I really wanted to enjoy what time I had left to just be a kid.

Daddy was in one of his moods, though, and I suspect that woman he knows was part of it. Mom told me all about that woman

when she gave me the speech about sex and
life and marriage when I was fourteen.

"Men have problems with their bodies,"
she said, looking only a little embarrassed.
"They all cheat. It's just something we put up
with if we can. It's nothing about love. Don't
even think that. It's just their biology. They
have their good sides and their bad sides. And
there are plenty of bad women, too," she
added. "Like *that woman*."

That woman lived in Brooklyn, in a brown-
stone that my father had bought for her in the
1970s. I took the subway out to it once, and
stood on the steps in front, looking through the
windows. That woman had a nice chandelier
and some paintings on the walls, but it was a
fairly plain house in Park Slope. I sort of think
I saw a little of her, too, walking up the street.
She wasn't even pretty, which was sort of what
amazed me. She wasn't like my mother. She
was tall, with big feet, and red hair that
needed some kind of style. Her face was
nothing like my mother's, nothing like the
women I knew, she looked Irish, I guess, she
looked sort of round and plain.

I don't really know if it was that woman I
saw, but I suspect it was.

So, just after high school graduation, I was
all ready to go to the island, but Daddy was

moody and told me I needed to stay because of Jimmy, who was supposed to have been in town.

All right, Jimmy McTeague.

He's a tennis player who goes to Wimbledon every year, he's practically a national champion, and his father owns McTeague Sports, the chain, although I never understand why they don't have stores in Manhattan.

I met Jimmy when he was at Exeter, at some dance, and I was just thinking he was cute. Marnie called him the Leech for some reason which I didn't quite understand, but I knew there was something interesting about him. He lived a different life than me, and I never really saw myself with that Midwestern jock-type. He was always sweating, too, which I guess goes with the whole athletic thing, but it's not something that's pleasant to be around an hour after a match.

Still, by the time I was seventeen, I really liked Jimmy. And no, I had no thoughts of marriage or anything like that. We hadn't actually even been intimate or anything, just held hands a lot and went to dances and out to dinner.

When I debuted, Jimmy shared the drudgery of that awful debutante season by being my escort; when I was really pissed off over not getting into my top college choice, Jimmy actually flew in from the West Coast— where he had some important tennis match— and took me out to dinner. Then, the night after I would normally go to the island, Jimmy told me we could sail there in this little boat he kept in Greenwich at the club.

That first night on the boat, I became a woman. Well, that's what he said. Sort of annoying that he said it. Not like I was a little girl ten minutes before. But boys are annoying sometimes.

Maybe I shouldn't have had the wine. Or maybe I'm glad I did.

We drank too many glasses of Chardonnay and one thing led to another.

Jimmy was never very aggressive before that. He was kind of shy that way. So I pretty much had to seduce him, but once we both closed our eyes and let our bodies take over, we knew how to make love.

And it really was love. It really was. I felt it.

At least it was that first time.

We spent that first night on the boat. We got into the harbor at about twelve or one in the morning and just slept together in the little bed. He snored sweetly. Not a hacking or sawing snore, but like a puppy dreaming. He did say something funny to me in the morning, something that struck me as odd, something about how maybe we could think about the future more now that we'd "mated."

I laughed at him when he said "mated." Sounded a hundred years old to say that. Or like we were animals in a zoo. I wondered if he couldn't say the more basic terms for sex.

He got a little angry when I laughed.

All right, I knew that maybe there would be trouble with Owen when I saw him on the jetty when we got off the boat the next morning. He looked like he'd been waiting there all night.

Like he'd been watching us.

The little turd.

He really was.

I care a lot for him, of course. We've known each other since we were both kids. He's the son of the gardener. His mother sometimes helps out with parties and laundry and other things.

He's cute, which helps, too, because although I have nothing against boys that aren't very good-looking, there's something about a good-looking one that just makes you want him around all the time.

So I'm barely dressed, some tacky beach towel around me basically, and there's Owen at the shore seeing both of us coming up from the boat and the first thing he says to me is, "What happened?"

I felt all nervous and even giggly, like I needed a cigarette. I told him I didn't want to see my mother for a day or two.

And then Jimmy just took over, like he always does. He has this way with guys—he always gets them on his side. Jimmy gave him a nickname and acted like Owen was Jimmy's kid brother and they just seemed to get along fine. It was like they'd known each other all their lives, in about five minutes. Owen seemed to like all the ribbing and you know, that sort of adolescent boy-talk they do. You know that. That way boys have of getting together and sort of sparring, and talking, and noticing each other's hair, or how one of them is sad, and they either peck it to death or get all brotherly. I saw it with Jimmy and his best friends at Exeter, too. The way they played like puppies. That's just what it was like—like watching two golden retrievers wrestle over a bone.

I didn't see Owen much during June. I guess he got the job down in town. Sometimes I saw him when we went to the Salty Dog, but he never waited on our table.

Jimmy was virtually attached at the hip

with me, which can get annoying no matter how much you care for a guy. I used to try and lose him in the mornings after he'd go off to play his beloved tennis with one of the local pros or with my mother. My mother is excellent at sports, which are pretty much not my thing. I like golf a little, and sometimes I like to swim, but the whole girl-jock thing is beyond me.

So Jimmy would slip out of bed and I'd get dressed and go down to visit Marci and Elaine, or maybe Elaine's brother, Cooper, down island.

Sometimes we'd take whole afternoons just having brunch, or wandering the Cove by Big Salt Pond.

Jimmy would get all pissed off at me. He was a little jealous. Well, a little more than jealous.

He thought that since he was the first guy I'd slept with, he somehow should've had more ownership of me. Or maybe I should've been more attached to him. I mean, I *was* attached. And he was *technically* the first guy I'd slept with, although I let Ricky Hofstedter press his fingers up there sophomore year, and then there was that time that I got drunk at Hollis Ownby's party and wound up making out with Harvey Somebody. He *was* a

Somebody. I just can't remember his last name.

But Jimmy had all these needs and some days, particularly in June and early July, I just wanted to chill and hang out with some friends without worrying about whether I was paying attention to Jimmy and all his issues.

I didn't think of Owen much, except sometimes I remembered how fun he was when I was younger and exploring the beaches; or how I'd take him out in one of my dad's small boats while he'd tell me all about his future plans. How he was going to start investing in stocks. I'd ask him how? And he'd look at me funny, and laugh. Then, he'd tell me how his mother's father had been well off and then when he turned twenty-one, he'd come into some trust fund.

I knew he was lying but I sort of liked his lies. They made the days go by. Sometimes the summer seemed short when I was around him, and by the time I got back to school in the fall, I felt renewed. I owed a lot of that to Owen.

But this summer, I've been distant from everybody. Part of it is Jimmy. And yes, it's sexual, I guess. But since I'm paying you by the hour, I'd guess that you're okay with me telling you, right?

Well, Jimmy seems to not be all that

aggressive in bed anymore. I know that must sound weird since I'm not terribly experienced in that arena, either, but I've watched movies, I've read books, and I talk with my girlfriends about this stuff. This isn't like twenty years ago when no one ever talked about sex. My friends all say their boyfriends seem to put the moves on them constantly.

With Jimmy, I have to literally reach down and grab him. And then, he just sort of, you know, touches me here and there and then he—well, you know—and then it's over and sort of unpleasant even though it's not ghastly or anything. It's just not what I expected.

And then there was that fiasco with my birthday party. Christ, it was embarrassing. Mind if I light up? I'm hungry for nicotine at the moment.

Ah, that's better. I know everyone has to give up smoking at some point in their lives, but how nice to not have to give it up just yet.

So, the 17th was my big party, and I didn't even want Owen there—he didn't fit in with Jimmy's friends. Most of my friends found him a little cold.

Plus, there was the whole problem of his mother, who's a force to be reckoned with. She's always looking at me like I'm the Whore of Babylon. She was helping us set up the party but she kept giving me that look.

You know that look.

That mother look.

But when Owen showed his face I was happy to see him. It was sort of a relief to finally because he definitely is nice to me no matter what. And I barely saw him this summer. Well, I saw him when he went swimming.

In our pool of course. In *our* pool. A whole ocean out there and he has to be in our pool.

I called him Leech (funny that he and Jimmy both have been called that, huh?) when he wasn't around because he really is such a leech. I mean it in a funny nice way, not some awful way. I once slipped off a rock into one of the little ponds on the property, and my legs were covered with leeches. They don't hurt. You'd be surprised at that, wouldn't you? You'd think something that sucks your blood would hurt, but they don't. It's just the fact they're there that makes them bothersome.

So it was my little joke: calling Owen "Leech." I care a lot for Owen, actually. We grew up together practically. My island boy. My father laughs whenever I call Owen a leech behind his back but my mother, well, she doesn't understand that kind of humor. That ironic kind of humor. I mean it as an affectionate term.

Sort of like the way Jimmy calls him Mooncalf. It's a name.

I guess it distances me from him or something. But it does get annoying when someone is always borrowing things or using your things or assuming things just because his father works in the garden. I like them. They're like family. I feel a lot for Owen, but really, he should've gotten over that Leech thing years ago.

I can hear my mother's voice in my head: "That's cruel, Jenna."

I get accused of cruelty all the time. Not physical cruelty. My mother means it's cruel to fault poor people for using our things.

My mother has this thing for Owen. Well, for all young men. She won't acknowledge it, and she thinks Daddy's the bad one, but I know she likes the boys who hang around me. And no, I'm not jealous of her. Why should I be? She's old. Her time has come and gone. My time is only just beginning.

Anyway, school boys do not want forty-year-old women. It's embarrassing, really. Even at the party, Mom is sauntering around in that green getup she has that looks too glitzy for the island. We all go casual here, so she looked too done up. *Too* too, as Missy Capshaw says. She's *too* too.

Missy came down from the Vineyard for the party. Shottsy had his cousin Alec with him, and pretty much the whole gang showed up except for the Faulkners who all went to Maine for the summer.

I guess a bunch of my other friends came, and then six or seven of Jimmy's, and then Owen with his shirt that was so new it still had the wrinkles from the cardboard box. Shottsy made a big point of letting everyone know that part of the plastic liner was still under the collar.

Owen brought me this nice little gift. I mean that in an ironical way.

That's really the issue here. What he brought.

I was enjoying some margaritas and just getting sort of high and Marnie regaled me with that story again, the one about her brother's professor and how he and two female students had gone off to Fenwick together and then got caught in the worst way, the very worst way possible.

That's when I saw what Owen was doing.

I saw that he had already cast a spell. Some kind of spell. Just like a witch.

Over Jimmy.

I saw Jimmy put his hand in Owen's hair. I noticed how they laughed together over a private joke.

I know it must seem irrational and paranoid, but the first thing I thought was:

That island bastard is trying to steal my boyfriend.

You can imagine how I felt. I mean, I thought it was ludicrous. It wasn't like Skippy Marshall and that Donovan character from Harrogate School—they were both obvious homosexuals. We all knew about it since they got into the drama club and developed the perfect butts in the workout room doing squats.

This was different. I thought it was absolutely ludicrous. But I became livid as I watched them. Absolutely *livid*.

Working on my third or fourth margarita, I cast sidelong glances over at the two of them. Missy kept talking and Alec kept eyeing my breasts like the stupid jerk he could be. I had my little circle, but they knew something was up, too. They knew that Jimmy did not fawn on me, and I didn't really enjoy that.

I suppose if I had not been drinking, I wouldn't have caused a scene.

But I kept my eye on the two of them, and I saw the touches.

Yes, that's right. *Queerish little touches*. Not the kind that boys do. Not normally.

Owen touched Jimmy's elbow, and Jimmy looked at Owen's hand. They laughed. Whenever one of them could, he took his fist and gently patted the other on the chest.

Like old chums? Yes, sure, maybe. Certainly that's what I'd like to believe, but in fact, I saw Jimmy show him more genuine attention, not that needy attention he showed me, but the kind of attention every girl wants but never gets from a boy.

That adoration kind of attention.

And Owen *milked* it.

I asked Marnie later on. She said I was imagining things, that Jimmy had been bedding girls since eighth grade, that it was just that boy thing. That's what she said: "That prep-school boy thing where they get together and they touch each other and they tell dirty jokes and they check each other out. It's because they both want you. They need to figure out the competition."

But I don't know.

I stood there, feeling embarrassed and humiliated, and at *my* party.

At my own party.

Finally I couldn't stand it.

Jimmy leaned forward and whispered

something to him. It was like slow motion. I can remember it now like it's happening right in front of my face over and over again.

I saw his lips move as he whispered. Owen leaned into him. Jimmy's hand rested on Owen's shoulder. Maybe I was hallucinating or maybe I saw what I saw, but I think Jimmy McTeague placed the barest whisper of a kiss on Owen's ear, at my party, with me watching, with me having to bear witness to it.

God, it's so gothic. It's so...*Provincetown*.

It really hit me hard. I began crying, without knowing I was doing it, weeping, just standing there.

Alec took my hand and said, "Aw, princess, what's up?"

I shook myself free of that crowd and walked right over to those two horrible boys, that horrible Jimmy McTeague.

"If you embarrass me here, I will destroy you," I whispered.

And then, of course, I had to go back to my party. I *had* to. I was obligated to all my friends. I was not going to let the boy who'd been sleeping with me for nearly two months humiliate me in front of everyone.

It wasn't until the next morning that I opened the gift that Owen had given me.

That's pretty much why I freaked out with my usual panache.

I didn't want to see Owen again.

Ever.

But I knew Jimmy would still be mine no matter what we both went through together.

After all, remember these things: The happiest people don't necessarily have everything. They just make the most of everything that comes their way. Sometimes good things come out of a good cry. You can't base how you'll feel about tomorrow on what today brings.

When I think of all I've had to deal with, particularly with Jimmy, these sentimental thoughts bring me comfort. Even if they're off some greeting card somewhere.

Oh yeah, what Owen gave me for my birthday.

It was a gun. A crap-ass gun at that. It was tiny. It had some pearly kind of handle and the safety looked like it had rusted out.

I doubted that it even worked.

I thought it was a joke at first, but I guess not.

It looks like something you'd buy from some little old lady in Brooklyn, some little old lady with a thousand cats and one of those old

fox furs who chain-smokes and lives in a studio
she's had since the 1950s.

Still, it was a gun, and I have to admit,
that's the creepiest thing he could've given me.

He scares me a little.

I mean, what kind of psycho gift is that?

AFTER A PARTY

Jimmy grabbed Owen's elbow, laughing, the smell of beer and tequila mixed in the air.

Owen giggled, too, and said, "Let's go to the jetty. It's beautiful there. You can see the North Star."

"You know the North Star?"

"Yeah. I know all the stars. I'm an islander. I know the Dippers and Scorpio, too."

"You're such a Mooncalf with all the stars in your pocket," Jimmy said, his grin big and goofy and not that of the controlled jock he'd once seemed. "God I wish I knew the stars like you. I want to just—just—look at the stars and know which ones they are, and where the earth is in relation to them. You can show me all of them. We can go out night sailing sometime. I would love that, wouldn't you? You can really see the constellations when you get away from all this. You could tell me all of them, all their stories, all night."

The party spun around them, and Owen sensed that Jenna glared at his every move.

She'll understand, he thought. *Eventually.*

"Maybe Jenna can come, too."

"Why? She can be a bitch," Jimmy whispered. "She and her friends and half these people here. All these quote-unquote friends of mine, of hers, who are they? Damn it, who are they? And Jenna. Christ. Jenna. She doesn't know me. She doesn't know you."

"So just you and me," Owen said. "Want to go down to the jetty? We can see the stars there, too."

"God yeah, show me the stars," Jimmy said, and he kept saying it over and over again as they stumbled their way down the path along the bluffs.

Every now and then Owen stopped and let Jimmy take his hand.

Jimmy's hand was warm, and above them, the sounds of the party faded, and the smell of pine and sea mingled.

The moon cut a path for them all the way to the jetty.

By the time they got there, Jimmy had

already grabbed Owen and pulled him close until their chests pressed together, their thighs met.

Jimmy brought his lips to Owen's mouth.

VOICES IN THE DARK:

"It's all right, I know you. I know what we both want."

"Shut up. Just shut up."

"Come here. Come here. Let me help you. It's all right. It feels good."

"No, not like this. No."

"I've been so lonely."

"Oh."

"Wanting this."

"Oh."

"Since the first time I saw you."

"Oh."

"Does this feel good?"

"Ah."

"Will you let me take you?"

"Oh."

"Ask me."

"Oh."

"Ask me."

"Owen, take me? Owen? Take me."

OWEN

I had found my way to Jenna. It wasn't much different than kissing a girl. Once I allowed Jimmy to feel as if he needed to seduce me, that I might be the unwilling partner, it was easy to hold his attention because he liked resistance. I could feel it as he held me. He wanted me to try and pull away.

He told me to close my eyes and pretend he was a girl, to just let him do things to me, to just keep the image of a beautiful girl in my mind while he did things.

Jenna's was the only face I saw.

I knew that once I had Jimmy McTeague of the Ivy League in my arms, once I had pushed myself into him, owned him, dominated him…Jenna would be mine.

I look at the boy that I was then:

Owen Crites. Mooncalf. He mounts the rich boy and drives his point home.

And no, I'm not gay.

I got no thrill from what I did to Jimmy McTeague, how I made him feel tenderness and acceptance and release that night.

It felt less like sex to me than stabbing someone over and over while they curled around you.

I caressed him as no one ever had, to the point that he wept against my chest.

It was purely because I thought of Jenna. My love for her.

Love is purity.

My next decision, as I lay there with that puppy whimpering his soul into my ear, was just how I was going to murder him.

THE LAST OF SUMMER

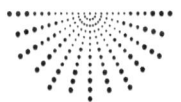

JIMMY MCTEAGUE KEEPS A DIARY

Dear Diary, as they say:

    1. Need to train better. Wake up an hour earlier every morning. Run two miles. Then practice. Then row.

    2. July was a waste. Feeling like I'm getting lazy. More strength training. Check out the sucky gym in town.

    3. Jenna's a bitch. She thinks she knows. She doesn't know. She'll never really know.

    4. Need to get back with Jenna. Need to figure this out.

    5. I can't resist him. It's awful what we're doing. But I know I can stop. I know if I just stick with the program I can stop. I think he's evil.

    6. What we did was wrong. I know that. What Jenna and I can build is right.

7. Call the Padre and Madre for more money.

8. Become a better person. Quit all the lying. Lying is bad. There's no reason. If you feel the way you feel, let it all out. Don't keep holding it in. Doesn't matter what Dad thinks. Doesn't matter if you know what you need from life. You can let it out. Other people do. Other people need those things, too.

9. Maybe it's not real. Maybe it's just sex. Maybe I shouldn't let it happen. But now all I think about is him.

10. Jenna and Mooncalf.

11. Mooncalf.

12. He told me something really smart. Just shows that you don't need all these prep schools and universities to be smart. He said, "Love is purity." It is so true. It's something I couldn't say out loud. But it's so true. But there's more to life than love. You can't survive on love. You can't have the important things in life just because of love. No one pays for three houses and European vacations and clothes from Italy and Rolls-Royces with love.

MY NAME'S JIMMY MCTEAGUE. It's safe to

assume you know that because you are me sitting here reading my diary. Since, after all, no one else is going to read this if I can help it.

It's also probably safe to assume that you'll burn these pages someday to make sure no one else reads them. But for now, writing it down seems right. My favorite movie is probably still the *Little Mermaid*, which I saw when I was nine years old, and I still watch it once a year at least. Why? Because it's about sacrifice for what you want. I've always sort of believed in that. My dad doesn't understand why I watch a cartoon to inspire me. Sometimes I watch it before a match because it gets me going. I don't see why being smart and grown up has anything to do with abandoning the things you believed in when you were a kid.

I've wanted to keep a diary since I was about nine, about the same time as I saw that movie, but I didn't start till I was twelve and then I threw it all out. So after another brief attempt at sixteen, I've decided now that I'm about to enter Harvard, it's time for me to keep one. I'm not only about tennis, anyway. I get tired of that dumb jock image. My SATs were through the roof. I get good grades and I'm totally wrapped up in Medieval history, which I figure I might pursue even after I graduate. If I graduate. If I make it through. If all the bad things that I've found out about don't happen in the meantime, and it all ends.

This part of the diary is about my summer. Jenna and I were having a great year together, although I wasn't always there for her, I suppose, because of the matches I had in England and out in California, and then she spent spring break in Aruba, so that last week in May was really our first full week together, which is why I took the *Karenina* out of the yacht club and we sailed lazily up and down the coast for a few days.

I was so pissed off at Dad over a lot of things. First and foremost was the talk he gave me, about how I needed to uphold the family and how I needed to look at life differently, not as a kid but as someone who had responsibilities and wanted to live a certain way with certain kinds of people.

I didn't forget about Chip, but I guess that's one of those things I have to put aside. My dad says so anyway.

Chip was annoying anyway, and the time we spent together wasn't very meaningful because the whole time I kept thinking to myself: where will this go? Two guys can't marry. I'll lose everything.

And Chip was all about loins, anyway. And

he wanted me all the time. I like a bit of chase. I don't want someone who always wants me. What's the fun in that?

I shouldn't even write about it here. What if someone finds out? I'm not really gay anyway, I just get in these situations. I suppose I fall in love with people. And of course, the animal needs. They take over, don't they? Everyone's like that. You see someone pretty and you just want them.

Chip turned out bad. All that mess about fighting and arguing and him claiming I broke his arm when I didn't break it and if he fell it was his fault anyway for standing in my way and not letting me pass. He did that sort of blackmail thing too, but I showed him I wasn't going to put up with that kind of shit.

I fell for Jenna pretty hard.

I mean, who wouldn't?

She's gorgeous and full of life and her brain is just amazing.

And the money. To pretend it's not there is like not noticing her bra size.

All the guys seem to want her. I really had to fight off that bulldog with the Ferrari from Choate, but it wasn't too hard to dazzle her on the courts. She's a big fan of tennis, which helps, and that night we went for a walk back in the city really turned things around for me.

I mean, we were walking down Fifth Avenue, and she was talking about what she wanted from life, all the wonderful things, to see the world and experience the best of everything and how her trust fund was huge and she intended to always have the life her parents had…and my mind was turning a hundred little things around. I was walking with her under cloudy skies and I was thinking about how this was right.

Being with Chip was wrong because it was based on that one thing, that physical thing, the urge I had that took me over when he was under me.

I thought, all right, I know where this will go with Jenna. We'll marry, we'll have children, we'll build something really solid.

She has all this family land and properties and I'm really good at handling investments, so we'll be perfect together. She'll look right for business, too. And she wants kids really badly. So badly that she's not all that interested in college.

I suspect she wants to just get out from under her parents and be on her own and make her own life.

She has millions from her grandmother and it's earning more millions every year, she said, so why should she have to go through college? She wanted to do some magazine work, one of those high fashion magazines and her family has huge pull in that area and she was smart enough.

It hardly bears comparison with a night spent on a dirty mattress in the back of some studio apartment in Chelsea with Chip, who fell on hard times after prep school.

That sleaziness he had, like an air, like marijuana smoke in the back of a bus—that's what his place was like. He was slumming; degrading himself. His parents had cut him off, and he was willing to live like that. Hardly any furniture, a job that barely paid him per month what a reasonable man can live on. And still, he was willing to live like that for the sake of the feeling in his dick.

I am never going to let that happen to me. I am never going to let people know how I am on the inside if I can help it. I got so mad at Chip I guess I ended up roughing him up a little, but he kept trying to ruin things, and I just won't let anyone do that. My dad is ruining things as it is, and pretty soon other people are going to know how he's ruining things, and I do not intend to be in that spot with him.

I remember clasping Jenna's hand while I listened to her go on about the life she intended for herself. So I knew that if I just kept my eyes on her, it would all go in the right direction. When we made love for the first time, it even felt right. She was overheated on the inside, it was like lava or something, it felt so natural.

I thought it would all turn out all right.

Until I met Mooncalf.

I tried to fight it, too. I looked at him and tried. I tried not to look at his body. So well developed. The way he spoke, almost sullenly. The fit of his khakis. The smile when it comes up, finally. Even his toes sticking out from his sandals.

Don't ever say someone can't fall in love through the eyes, because those blue eyes of his just grabbed me and held me the first time we met.

I didn't want him then, but I knew this guy had it in him to take me over.

And I suppose he already did that.

There's even a dangerousness to him I enjoy. I find myself looking over Jenna's shoulder, when we're at the beach, or bicycling, hoping he's there, just out of reach.

And then, the party. It was like waking up for the first time. It was like knowing that I'd been telling myself lies for years. That I'd been foolish and wrong. Now, all I think about is

Mooncalf and I wish we were in a different world, not one of secrets and half-truths, but one where we could just be together. I know he feels the same.

I'm pretty much sleeping on the boat now. I can't stay with Jenna.

Not in her room.

And her dad gives me those looks, which aren't pleasant, either. Jenna's been cold. Can't blame her.

I know somehow it will all turn out okay. I know it will because I know life is not meant to be bad or confusing. If we can all just get through this summer, it'll somehow work out because life is supposed to work out.

Sometimes, I get so lonely I want to just hold someone. Even Jenna.

As a friend.

I want to see Mooncalf again, but he's been avoiding me since the party. I've had two weeks now, seeing Jenna and her family, playing a little golf, some tennis, taking the boat out when I can. Jenna's been good about this even if she's turned icy. She seems to handle my silences well. She really is a friend. I'm glad we can be this close and that she can be so understanding. Most of the time, she seems to act as if the night of her party never happened, as if I didn't go off with him.

She won't really understand what it means, anyway. She'll think she'll know, but I'll let her know it was nothing.

I'll get her thinking about us again, which is what she really wants, anyway.

A HURRICANE APPROACHES

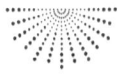

here he is again:
I see him. That boy Owen. He's been running along the beach, swimming too much for his own good, working on his oxygen intake because breathing is the key. He has felt an unexpected strength grow within him to match his body's power.

THE WEEKS after the party went in a blur of moments and flashes in Owen's brain—the sky clouded and then became unbearably sunny, the humidity soared and then dropped and then soared again; a tropical storm to the south had been upgraded to a hurricane but it would not strike so far north as Outerbridge.

One night, Owen lay in bed convinced he'd heard a gun go off somewhere on the island.

August was like that sometimes.

"OWEN. WHY?"

"Why *what?*" he asked, shielding his eyes from the sun.

Jenna had emerged from the wooden deck all wrapped in a big yellow towel; to him it was as magnificent as a summer dress.

The smell of the pool was intoxicating. He had just finished his morning laps and felt clean and strong.

He wanted to kiss her. He thought of what it would be like to touch her. They stood so close.

"What kind of birthday present was that?"

"It's just a pistol. An antique."

"Why?"

"I thought you'd want it. I thought you'd like it."

"I'm not a fan of guns."

"No one is. But it has that inlay. It seems feminine."

"You must be out of your mind. To give me that as a gift. On my birthday."

"It was my grandfather's."

"Well, I'm giving it back. God, I don't want it in the house, let alone in my hand."

"You need protection."

"From what?"

"Jimmy," Owen said. He sucked a breath in briefly. It was time to let it begin.

He felt a curious shiver sweep through his body, as if he were on the verge of some delightful pleasure.

"He told me…"

"Told you what? What did he say? Was it about me?"

He wanted to make sure that she was completely focused on him. On his lips as he spoke.

"No, it's nothing. I just think you should keep the gun."

"No, he said something," she nearly snarled. "Tell me."

"I'm sure he didn't mean it," Owen said.

"It made you think I needed a gun?" Her face went blank. She looked down at her feet for a moment. Then, she glanced up and looked him in the eye. "What's been going on between you two?"

"Nothing," Owen whispered.

"Owen, what's going on?" she said.

He took a deep breath before speaking again.

"Jenna, I want you to be safe. That's all. Look, I know you don't care for me, and that's fine. I can't make you like me. And I know I can't make you…care for me…in a way I happen to care for you. No one is magician enough for that. I've thought about you since we were both little kids. I've always considered you someone special."

"*What?*" she asked in a voice that was barely more than a mouse squeak.

"I know that you'll go on to some really great college and you'll meet lots of guys like Jimmy and you'll come back to the island during the summer and be friendly with me but you'll see me as the townie who paints houses for a living, or maybe works on boats. And you'll have a different life."

"What is this all getting to—" Jenna gasped, and then her eyes lit up. "You lost the island accent. You talk like one of us now."

She said it as if it was one of the most dreadful things imaginable.

"That isn't true," Owen said. He glanced away, looking to the house and the beginnings of the roses his father so lovingly tended.

"This makes no sense. I don't want that gun."

"I know I'm nothing to you, Jenna. But please just consider keeping the gun as some kind of protection. Jimmy is not who he seems. I've seen a side of him...well, I've heard him say things...I just think you need to have that gun just in case."

He turned and walked away, his body barely dry from the swimming pool.

She called after him.

He walked from the pool to the back lawn and disappeared down the path.

ANOTHER MORNING, he helped Mr. M with his golf clubs and luggage, driving the truck up from the ferry. Mr. M had almost missed summer on the island.

"Business takes a man over," he told Owen on the way up the hill to the house. Mr. M was the biggest man Owen had ever seen—like a bear, but slick, too, and shiny. He had on dark glasses and a rumpled blue oxford cloth shirt. His skin was like pink snow as if he never allowed himself more than a minute or two per day in sunlight.

When Owen got to the door with the last of the bags, Mrs. M (he had to start thinking of her as Cathy if he was going to ever grow up) kissed her husband lightly on the nose.

"How's the summer?"

"Quiet," Mrs. M said.

"Where's that boy?"

"Which?"

"McTeague," Mr. M said.

"I think it's over. She's gone to Dr. Vaughan three times in two weeks. That's a record for her," Mrs. M said, and then turned to Owen. "Sweetie, would you mind picking up the mail for me?"

Owen nodded, feeling far too obedient, his heart beating too fast, too much within his frame, as if his muscles were about to twist and untangle; he was afraid for a moment that he had not heard what he thought he'd heard.

OWEN SAT by the koi pond, absorbing the last of an afternoon sun on one of his days off—the weather had gone back and forth, between brief bouts of showers and then sudden sunbursts. He was about to reach for Dagon beneath the placid green water, when he noticed a shadow reflection move across the water.

He didn't turn, but knew that Jimmy had come up behind him.

"Aren't you ever going to talk to me again?"

Owen shrugged.

"I thought...I thought we could...we could at least be friends," Jimmy said. "I think about you. All the time."

"Don't come here again." Owen measured his words carefully.

The shadow withdrew and Owen had the sun to himself again.

OWEN LAY back in the grass and closed his eyes.

As the violet darkness of his inner mind grew, he began to see the shadow sea of Dagon's realm. From the dusky waves, a form emerged, a magnificent sea god, its eyes round and without mind, like those of a shark, its body slick as oil with thousands of fins sprouting along its back; and as it grew, Owen knew what the god asked of him.

"I SAID PEEL THE POTATOES," his mother said, but he could see the look in her eyes. She wouldn't look directly at him. His mother was afraid of him. A little. Just a little fear.

That was good.

"Don't use that tone of voice with me," Owen said almost politely, as he lifted the first potato and brought it to the small sharp knife.

"Something's missing in the house," she said, but his mother had begun saying strange things the past few weeks—sentences that didn't go together, phrases that meant something only in her mind.

"You probably misplaced whatever it is," he told her almost nonchalantly. "You've always been like that, haven't you?"

WHEN STORMS COME TO OUTERBRIDGE, they usually have lost most of their power, they usually have been downgraded from hurricanes when they hit Bermuda to tropical storms when they reach Long Island, and by the time they make it past Block Island and start heading to the Avalons, it's usually high winds and warm rains but not much damage. The islanders who are over sixty remember

the storm of '53 that "took the hats off houses," as they said, and generally made a mess of
the summer homes.

The storm that arrived the last week of
August was not a terror, nor did it threaten to
take the hats off houses. It was a warm palace
of rain and wind and it changed the geometry
of the island with its shifts and movements.

The sky became a hardened gray and the
rain constant while the koi pond overflowed.
Owen ran outside with his father, newspapers
curled over their heads, to try and save the fish
as they flip-flopped along the mud and grass,
their patchwork colors seeming to melt
beneath the downpour.

OWEN WAS on his way to work, using his
father's truck to get to the Salty Dog, when he
saw the figure standing in the pouring rain of
afternoon down by the docks. Owen pulled
the truck to the edge of the road and parked.
He got out in the rain, opening his dark
umbrella. The smell of fish was overpowering
—it was a stink he was used to, but with the
storm it was worse.

Jimmy looked otherworldly: he wore a

shiny parka, and his face was pale beneath it. He nearly galloped over to Owen, and reached out to touch him on the shoulder, but Owen pulled back.

Owen slammed the truck door shut.

"I'm going to work," Owen said.

"Mooncalf?"

"Leave me alone."

"I thought you——"

"You thought wrong."

"I've been waiting for you. At the boat. Every night, I watch you leave the restaurant and walk home. Every night I wish you'd come to me."

"You disgust me."

"Stop it. I know that's not true." Jimmy's shoulders began heaving.

The sound of the rain became thunderous and sheets and blocks of it seemed to dump right down around them.

"God. God!" Jimmy cried out, his arms going up to the sky like some clown, like some revival preacher clown; the rain pouring against his face. A thunderclap hid the sound of his bleating. "If only you knew! If only you could grow up inside me! Knowing how I've been pushed and pulled, first my father forcing me into tennis and basketball and soccer since I was six years old, the camps I've gone to every summer, and these schools I go to, and what it all means when *inside*...inside, Owen... you know something about yourself that's like a doorway into a different world. Something that's like...I don't know...like a doorway out of this torture place and into this garden."

Jimmy's arms came down, and now he hung his head. The rain obliterated everything else and it was just the two of them left surrounded by a slate gray world.

"When I was a little kid I had this garden that I helped create," Jimmy said, still shouting but looking down at his shoes as he stepped closer towards Owen. "It had vegetables and flowers in it, nothing pretty and nothing special, but it was mine. My dad dug it up in the middle of the night. He dug it up and told me that no son of his was going to be a goddamn gardener."

Owen leaned forward into Jimmy, putting his hand on the side of his face and looking at the weeping boy, the rich boy who had nothing, all that wealth washing away in the storm.

"That's what this feels like," Jimmy said through heaving sobs, his voice growing smaller and smaller the closer Owen got. "Like someone is trying to dig up the garden I need to grow. And you know you need to go to that garden, but every single person, from your mother to your father to your coaches to your teachers to your friends to even strangers —every single human being—wants you to keep away from the one garden where you know you can just help things grow and where you'll feel calm for once in your life…where you feel that what you have known inside your body, inside your heart, inside your mind, is the way God and nature and whatever it is that moves things within any human being— meant for you to be."

Owen gasped when Jimmy finished.

"Jim, Jimmy, Christ, I know," Owen said, feeling as if he'd rehearsed the lines. He attempted a feeble smile. Part of him felt removed within his body. He was watching himself—Owen—react, seem gentle, seem kind. "It's just like that for me, too."

The rain began to let up as they stood there, Owen's hand feeling the heat of Jimmy's face as he cupped it. A vague sliver of sunlight broke free of clouds to the east.

Owen looked around at the tourists coming off the ferry, their black and clear and red and green umbrellas all blossoming above their heads, and there, beyond the crab shack were six of the island guys he'd grown up with.

"Look, we can't do this here," he said. "Get in the truck."

OWEN DROVE in silence through a rain-shattered world—and followed the slick black island roads until they were nearly to the Great Salt Pond. Jimmy seemed content with the quiet of the drive. When Owen glanced over, he noticed that Jimmy pressed his forehead against the window beside him, reminding him somehow of a puppy.

Finally, they came to the end-of-road break that looked out over the enormous pond.

When he'd turned off the ignition, Owen reached over and took Jimmy's hand.

"I know it's difficult," Jimmy said. "I'm not like this either. Not really. There are things I want out of life. Things that have nothing to do with this. But right now. Christ, right now, this is it."

"Other people can do this kind of thing, but I can't. It wouldn't be right."

"No, it wouldn't be. But we can go somewhere it'll all be all right. Somewhere no one can find us."

"Where?" Owen laughed. "Where would it be? My god. *Where*?"

Jimmy recoiled as if he'd been slapped. "Out to sea. In the boat."

"For how long, Jimmy? How long before your dad cuts you off or before we move on? What if this is all lust? What if this isn't meant to happen? How long before you need to go off to your Ivy League school and then marry and meanwhile, I live in some kind of shame on this island. I'm not like you. I'm not like the kind of men who do this with other men. I'm just… Just."

"Just?"

"Just not sure what I feel right now. It's confusing. You're all I think about." Owen modulated his breath, his voice, changing the tone to a husky, low growl as he spoke slowly and carefully. "I just want you. Just you. Not her. That's all I know."

It was easy to lie once Owen knew what he would do with Jimmy. How he would destroy him. How it would go smoothly once everything was in place.

"Oh, baby," Jimmy moaned, leaning over, into him, pressing his scalp against Owen's neck. Owen felt wetness along his throat. "You don't know how long I've hoped you'd say it."

"We don't need Jenna, do we? Or girls like her," Owen whispered. "God, if I could, I'd kill her."

"Who? Kill? *Owen?*"

"I didn't mean that," Owen said, and kissed him on the top of his head.

Owen knew that he had him now. He had Jimmy right where he wanted him.

Where Dagon wanted him.

DAGON

"**O**wen?" his mother asked, holding something in her hand before he could tell what it was.

The statue.

It had always seemed enormous to him, but in her hand, it was only about a foot long. The base was cracked, a few of its teeth had fallen out, and all that remained was a grotesque statue someone had once carved and left behind.

"Where'd you get that?"

"Right where you left it," she said. She hefted it in her hand. "Where'd it come from?"

"I…I found it."

"You found it?"

"Yeah, I did. It's mine."

He held his hand out.

"Did you buy it?"

"That's none of your business."

"Why put it in the fishpond?"

"It's an ornament. It looked nice there. Give it back."

"It's terrible looking. Its eyes. Whoever made this thing was sick. I think some kind of animal was used. It smells, too."

"Mother."

"Don't 'mother' me. You may be a young man, but you have a thing or two to learn. I know you, Owen. I know how you think. I saw you that morning."

"What are you talking about?"

"I saw you. You cut your arm and let it bleed on this…this thing."

"That's crazy. Why would I do something crazy like that? Like—what—like cut myself? And what—did you say—bleed?"

"It's some kind of awful thing, isn't it? This thing. It's some awful thing for you. The way your mind works."

She looked at the small statue in her hand, and then back to his face. She squinted as if trying to see him more clearly.

"You've never been quite right. You know how you're different from other boys, don't you? Yes, you're crafty and you look good in a suit and you can make your muscles talk for you. But I know you better than you know yourself, Owen Crites. I know how cold you are. I know how you believe different things than most people do."

He felt her closing in like a bird of prey as she moved toward him.

"What exactly *is* this thing? A toy? Is this something you talk to? Is this...is this...some kind of devil god? Do you worship graven images now?" She said it in a half-joking manner and that was the worst of it. She wasn't taking Dagon seriously.

Owen felt as if his tongue had been cut out. He felt a heat rash along his neck. He looked from the statue to his mother and back again.

Then, he grinned.

"Don't be ridiculous," he said. "You have such a small mind. You're quick to judge when you're the one with the cold heart. You set a trap for Dad, and now you punish him for that same trap. You can't even love your only child. And your imagination—your *paranoid* imagination—finding some carved art in a koi pond, something that you claim you watched me bleed over...Did you ever for a single moment think that maybe I hated myself so much I wanted to slit my wrists? But something made me stop. Something kept me from hurting myself. But it wasn't the thought of you, was it? It wasn't the love of my mother that saved me, was it? It was the thought that maybe one day I'd have a moment just like this. A moment when Dad is out of the house. A moment when you're at your worst. Do you know what I am going to do with you?"

"What are you talking about? Owen?"

"Give me that," he said, snatching it from her hand. "It's mine. Not yours."

She stood before him, trembling.

Owen cradled Dagon in his arms. He closed his eyes, and whispered a brief prayer.

When he opened them, he said, "Here's something I hope you think about until the moment you die. I am going to be your dutiful son for a long time. But the moment that I get an inkling you're old and feeble, I'm going to show up at your bedside one night. I will press my hands over your nose and mouth and smother you to death. And in those last moments, you'll look at me and know that everything you were ever afraid of came true. Every single fear you have right now."

His mother pressed her hands to her lips, unable to speak.

It was the power of Dagon, of course. It

was there, in the room. The god was there with him.

Dagon whispered within his blood: *You will die like the bitch that you are.*

Or had Owen himself said it aloud, in a whisper, to his mother?

THIS IS how it will happen, the voice came to him. *You will tell Jenna things. You will tell Jimmy some things. He harbors a madness. He is breakable. Then, she will kill him. You will save her. She will kill him and you will have her.*

He slept that night with Dagon next to him in bed.

He dreamed of the great realm beneath the sea. Owen no longer felt his age, but became a child again with Jenna beside him, the Queen of the Deepest Fathom.

"HELLO, SWEETIE," Mrs. M said.

She had just finished the Sunday cross-word puzzle, and looked up from the paper. "You all ready for four more days of this…this tempest?"

The kitchen was like a brilliant day compared to the murky rain outdoors.

Owen had come in through the back, his towel in his arms.

"Up for a swim, Cathy?"

Mrs. M shook her head. "Feeling a bit downtrodden from the rain. Ask Frank, he'd probably love a race with you."

"Mr. M's around?"

"Back and forth. Here for now."

"That's great. I would've thought with the rain…"

Mrs. M crossed her legs, one over the other. Owen thought for a moment that it was the most luxurious movement he had ever in his life seen.

"You here for Jenna?"

"I doubt she wants to see me."

"Owen," Mrs. M said, setting the paper down on the kitchen table. She arched an eyebrow. "Something's changed about you. What is it? Turn around."

Dutifully, he turned about and then back to face her again.

"You're different now. What's that all about?"

"Maybe it's my hair? It's getting long."

"No, that's not it." She smiled. "Are you in love?"

"No," he said, too quickly. "Maybe it's all the swimming."

"Well Jenna's in her room. She sleeps later and later. Go call her if you want. She should get up. It's nearly ten. No one should sleep this late. Not at her age. Not in summer."

Then, Mrs. M leaned forward.

"Between you, me, and the wall, Owen, I think she's really depressed over something. But I'm the last person she'll confide in. I imagine it's about a boy," she whispered. "That McTeague character."

Then, she said, lightly, "I always thought there was something not right about him."

"Oh. It's you," Jenna said.

She was sitting up in her bed, the covers around her white cotton nightgown.

"Hi," he said from the doorway.

The room smelled of sandalwood and vanilla.

"It's the rain. It does this to me," she said, pushing her hair back from her face. "I hate storms. I wish we were back in the city."

"I'm glad you're not."

"I'm just bored. Where's the sun? It's like

my summer got stolen. But you're my sun. You never fail to make me smile."

He stood there remembering the love he'd nearly forgotten. Why he care for Jenna so much. She was there for him, always. She had always been there for him.

"Okay if I come in? You know, like I used to?"

"Sure," she said, drawing her knees up. Then, "What is it between you two?"

He went into the bedroom, and sat down on the chair near her desk.

"Who two?"

"Don't be coy," she said. "Jimmy. Is it just sex?"

"Oh. That."

"Yes. That."

"I don't want to talk about it."

"I think you do."

"No, I really don't."

And then, something within him opened up.

It was like feeling a heat—a fire—in his chest, near his heart. It was Dagon. Dagon would inspire him. He felt that strength, suddenly, just when he thought he would falter.

Without even trying, tears poured from his eyes.

"Owen? Owen?" she asked, but he was nearly blind from the tears. She lifted the blanket, and patted a space next to her. "Come here. What's wrong? Owen?"

He bawled like a baby, and without knowing who—or what—had moved him, he found himself in her bed, her arms around him.

"Aw, Owen, what's wrong? What's wrong, my precious, precious, precious baby boy?"

She held him close, and Dagon was there. He felt it. He was not alone. Dagon was there. The voice that came from his throat didn't feel like his. It was some small boy's voice. Some crybaby who shivered and spilled emotion across the girl he loved.

"He...I didn't...I didn't want...I can't talk about...I didn't...he just kept...he just kept... he kept...he...I tried to...fight...fight... fight...push...hit...but...he just kept...he just kept...he just kept."

"Oh my god," Jenna said, her voice chilled and haunted. "No. He didn't. No. Did he? Owen? Did he *rape* you? Did he?"

"He just kept...oh god, Jenna, I can't face this...I wanted to...I wanted to...I wanted to...kill...myself...I wanted to..."

And so it began.

She said all the things she was meant to

say; and Owen told less than he needed to tell, because she made all the connections herself. He sat for hours in her arms.

Afterward, they made love.

HE WENT to the boat that night.

It was over now. It was all over.

He had won.

He wanted to take it to Jimmy. He wanted Jimmy to suffer from it.

If he could, he would've videotaped the afternoon, he would've tape-recorded Jenna's voice saying over and over again that she loved him, that it was all her fault, that Jimmy should never have come to the island, that he was bad, he was evil, and they should call the police, they should do something.

She even told him that if that bastard ever set foot on her property again, she would take that gun and shoot him right between the eyes.

The storm continued to rage across the gray expanse of sky. The Sound and the distant islands that could be seen were like watercolor images, fuzzy and melting.

Owen wore a bright yellow raincoat, a golden fire in the rain.

"Mooncalf, you look like a fisherman,"

Jimmy said. He wore cut-off jeans and a striped rugby shirt that was already soaked through, and his hair was like seaweed, hanging in his eyes. In his hand, a green bottle of beer. "Like, you know, a real New England Clam Chowder Fisherman!" He had to shout over a roll of thunder and a crack in the sky.

The world lit up for a moment and returned to gray.

Owen laughed, shaking his head. "You're drunk, boy."

"Want a beer?" Jimmy asked.

"Sure," Owen said. "How many you drink already?"

"Four. Maybe five. Who's counting?"

"Let's get out of the rain!"

"I like the jetty," Jimmy said, tossing him a small bottle just before he leapt to the dock.

He grabbed Owen's free hand. "No one's looking. We can hold hands, all right?"

"I don't know." Owen tugged away. He twisted the top off the bottle and took a swig. "God, I'm sick of rain!"

"Me, too!"

Jimmy tried to kiss him, but Owen stepped back to avoid it.

The rain lightened slightly; it was a warm rain; it washed across their bodies.

"She's sort of expecting us," Owen said.

"Who?"

"Jenna."

"Jenna?" Jimmy laughed, and then looked sidelong up the hill to the Montgomery place. "What for? I thought it was you and me tonight."

"She's...she's pissed. I guess that's what it is." Owen shrugged. "She's pissed and she wants us to talk to her. I told her."

"You...you *told* her?"

"After yesterday, in the truck, Christ, Jimmy, I can't not tell her. I've known her all my life. She's one of my closest friends. I told her about us. About how we're going to go away together. How you love me now. How everything's all right."

"You...you..." Jimmy stammered.

The bottle in his hand dropped to the rocky ledge, shattering.

"*You told her.*"

It was coming out now. The madness that they all had within them.

Owen wanted to smile, but knew that if he did, he would give himself away.

THE RAIN THINNED.

Minutes seemed to pass while Jimmy took

in what had just been said. Owen could practically see the thoughts in his eyebrows as they squiggled around, flashing anger and confusion, and the way he chewed his lip, and how his eyes wouldn't stop blinking.

Owen reached over and touched his scalp.

"Sometimes I think I see a halo around your head. I do. I think you're some kind of angel," Owen said.

"You fucking told her?" Jimmy growled. "You goddamn fucking son of a bitch told her what we've been…what we've…"

"Do you think she didn't see?" Owen set his bottle down on the jetty, and put his hands on Jimmy's shoulders, pulling him into him. "Do you think she's stupid? We're her friends. She can see. She told me she watched us that first night. She saw us. There was enough light to see our shadows, puppy. She told me it upset her, but she understood. She wasn't sure if it wasn't just one of those drunk boy things…or something else. I told her it was." Then, he added hesitantly, "Something else."

"You fucking goddamn son of a bitch gardener's son living in your goddamn peasant fucking world, you don't even know what you've done!" Jimmy shouted. His face had contorted until it was a mask of pain and fury.

"You fucking think that," spit flew from his

mouth, "that… that…you, you, with nothing to lose, can just throw what we have in front of her, in front of—you know what you're playing with? You're playing with things you can't even understand!" Jimmy began stomping around in a circle, alternating his shouts with lion roars.

When he finally quieted, Owen said, "What happened to yesterday? You looking up at God and telling me how this all felt, how you felt on the inside. How you felt you needed to let this out? What happened to that?"

"Don't you, you son of a bitch…don't use my words against me! I wasn't born to lose everything because I'm sleeping with some island townie whore, I wasn't born to have this get out, to have this ruin everything I've ever built."

"Listen to yourself. You talk like it's 1950. You won't lose everything just because…"

"You think so? You little *bitch*, you think I won't lose everything? You don't even understand what's going on here, do you? You think it's about me wanting you. Well, stakes are higher. I'll tell you something, boy: I want you, but I don't want you. You don't even understand why I have to be with Jenna, do you? Do you?"

Owen turned and began walking toward the strip of beach. Jimmy followed and kept right beside him.

"I don't want to hear about it," Owen said.

"Well, you need to. Maybe living in some little caretaker's house gives you zero perspective on this, but Jenna Montgomery means I will not be some poor shit like you."

Owen glanced back. "You're rich."

"Ha!" Jimmy cried. "You don't know the half of it."

"You're an heir to some fortune. Some sports store chain."

Jimmy shook his head. "It's not like it looks. My father has these stores. That's all he has. But the business is changing. It's changing, and he's had some setbacks. He's a terrible businessman, Mooncalf. All this stuff, this boat, the houses, all of it'll be gone in a few years. It's coming. He's going to be in jail someday, my father, and the IRS is going to eat him alive. And I don't intend to live like that. I do not intend..."

"Jesus," Owen gasped, and then began laughing. "You're just after her money."

Owen dropped to his knees on the wet sand.

"What's wrong with you?" Jimmy snarled, coming over to him. "You feeling bad now?"

"I actually thought you loved me," Owen said.

"It's not about whether I love you or not. It's not about that. But you've ruined even that now." He grabbed Owen under his armpits, lifting him up to a standing position. "You've destroyed something for me, Mooncalf. You really have."

Then, he looked up the hill to the house.

The lights were on in the pool area, and the upstairs light—Jenna's bedroom—was dim.

"I need to set this right," he said.

"No, don't, Jimmy, it's—"

"I need to," Jimmy said. "I'll tell her that it was weakness. I'll tell her I love her. I love her more than anything on the face of the earth. I'll tell her that I couldn't help myself with you, but that it was nothing. That you were nothing." He nearly laughed, but it had a cry within it. "You're just a little manipulative piece of trash. She'll understand. She's not like you. She'll understand."

Then, he took off in the rain, bounding up the wooden steps that crept like a vine along the side of the hill.

Owen waited two full minutes; an eternity. Then, he began taking the steps upward, but slowly. He waited along the top step, watching the house, seeing the light brighten in Jenna's room.

He heard the shots ring out before he reached the top step.

Soon dogs down in town were howling, and lights came up along the waterfront.

OWEN NOTICED the intense silence of the house as he stepped in through the doorway by the pool. He walked past the shimmering water to the kitchen.

He saw Mrs. M, lying in a pool of blood.

After that, Owen moved swiftly, his heart pounding.

Mrs. M resembled nothing of the mermaid or dragon or beauty she had once been. Death had robbed her of it. Blood took away the magic of her form.

Her eyes were open and fish-like.

Dagon, what is this? This isn't what was promised. This isn't what I prayed for.

He ran up the stairs to Jenna's room, and found *him* standing there, the gun in his hand—

On the bed, Jenna, bleeding, an enormous hole in her neck. Her hands moved as if she were trying to reach up to her neck.

She opened her mouth to cry out while blood pulsed from her throat.

He felt himself burning as he watched the last light flicker in her beautiful eyes.

Then, her eyes closed.

"MOONCALF, WHAT DID I DO?" Jimmy said, his skin red, his eyes narrow slits, his shirt torn and bloody. Tears and sweat shone like diamonds on his skin.

"What the hell did I do? I...I came up...I wanted to talk...and she...she had this..."

He held the pistol up.

"She...she threatened me...and then her mother came up...I grabbed it from her...I was going to leave...but they said things...her mother, too...they said things about me...and her father...About something...some lie... something you told her...something..."

"You killed them," Owen said as if even he didn't believe it.

"I guess so. It's kind of a blur. Funny thing is," Jimmy giggled in a way that seemed uncharacteristic, "the *funniest* thing is it didn't really feel like me at all. It felt like something else. Like I got taken over. Maybe if she hadn't pointed this gun. Maybe if I hadn't been drinking. I don't know. It happened fast. I was about to leave, but her mother saw me with the gun. She saw me and she was saying these things. And then I just wanted to shut her up and this thing was inside me. This feeling. Like something wanted me to point the gun at her mother. Just to scare her. And then: *kabang*."

"Jimmy?"

"Her father starts shouting upstairs and I feel this… this *wild thing* inside me. And I just go running back up the stairs and down the hall and there's her dad, and I think of my dad, and I think of all the things I'm never going to have, and suddenly the gun is going off, and then Jenna's screaming and she's picking up the phone in her room because I hear that beep beep noise and I have to stop her, I have to tell her not to call, that there'll be a way to work this all out. And then, I feel it in me again. I'm moving faster than I'm supposed to—the rest of the world is moving slow—and I'm in her room and she has a look on her face like she doesn't understand how I got there so quickly and I'm feeling this— power or something—and then I press the gun against her throat to shut her up."

Jimmy sighed, calming a bit. He pointed the gun directly at Owen. "It's something you

said to her. Isn't it? You said something terrible, didn't you?"

"Jimmy," Owen said. "Now, I know you're
upset. I know this is difficult right now. But I
want you to breathe. Take a few deep breaths.
Come on. Just breathe."

Jimmy looked at him curiously for a
moment, blinking, and then opened his mouth
to inhale.

Then, *out.*

Then, *in.*

Slowly, carefully.

BELIEF

I can look at this past summer now and see that it was all Dagon.

I summoned a terrible god into our world.

There is no madness except the madness of the gods. There is no purity except the purity of love.

Here is where he took me:

Down to the sailboat.

Out to sea.

WE SAILED along beside the cliffs and caves of Outerbridge Island, beyond the Montgomery Palazzo; the flashing of green and white from the lighthouse; north and then east we sailed, beyond the Great Salt Pond; out into a diamond night where sea met sky while a new storm howled through my mind, a storm beyond any hurricane that nature could send.

I felt as if I could barely breathe.

Jimmy held me down, gun to my head, calling me Mooncalf over and over again, speaking with tenderness, gazing at me with a drowning affection, his warm hand against my cheek, forcing me to whisper an incantation to Dagon of the purity and madness of human love.

"Mooncalf," he said. *"Mooncalf."*

GET STUFF. STAY CONNECTED.
READ MORE.

Visit DouglasClegg.com

DOUGLAS CLEGG

THE FACES

NEW YORK TIMES BESTSELLING AUTHOR

DOUGLAS CLEGG

MRS. BLUEBEARD

ABOUT THE AUTHOR

Douglas Clegg is the *New York Times* bestselling and award-winning author of *Neverland*, *The Priest of Blood*, *Afterlife*, and *The Hour Before Dark*, among many other novels, novellas and stories. His first collection, *The Nightmare Chronicles*, won both the Bram Stoker Award and the International Horror Guild Award. His work has been published by Simon & Schuster, Penguin/Berkley, Signet, Dorchester, Bantam Dell Doubleday, Cemetery Dance Publications, Subterranean Press, Alkemara Press and others.

A pioneer in the ebook world, his novel *Naomi* made international news when it was launched as the world's first ebook serial in early 1999 and was called "the first major work of fiction to originate in cyberspace" by *Publisher's Weekly*, covered in *Time* magazine, *Business Week*, *Business 2.0*, *BBC Radio*, *NPR*, *USA Today* and more. His book *Purity* was the first to be published via mobile phone in the U.S. in early 2001.

He is married, and lives and writes along the coast of New England.

Find the Author Online:
www.DouglasClegg.com

 facebook.com/DouglasClegg

twitter.com/DouglasClegg

www.ingramcontent.com/pod-product-compliance
Lightning Source LLC
Chambersburg PA
CBHW031124210626
46816CB00016B/2350